Revenge of the Witch

Crypt Witch cozy paranormal mystery series - book 3

K.E. O'Connor

K.E. O'Connor Books

REVENGE OF THE WITCH

ISBN: 978-1-915378-01-9

Written by: K.E. O'Connor

Chapter 1

"There's one of the little imps!" My sister, Aurora Crypt, pointed to a sickly green vapor as it slid from a crack in the cemetery.

I shook my head. Only Aurora would call a potentially lethal, soul sucking demon an imp.

"I'm on it." I raced over, stick in hand, and slammed it on the head of the demon who was trying to escape the prison.

"There's another creeping through here," Aurora yelled.

As I turned, she slammed her own stick on top of a demon's horned head before sealing the crack with a blast of white magic.

It was unusual for me to work a shift at the cemetery, but the resident demons were being tricky. They'd been disrupting the stability of the prison for almost a week, launching relentless attacks on any weakness they discovered. The whole family was working overtime to ensure none of them crept out and caused chaos.

The sticks we held weren't your average sticks, but powerful magic staffs that weakened demons by absorbing their energy when they came into contact with them.

"This is like a game of whack a mole, just with demons." Wiggles, my mostly faithful talking hellhound, wandered over with a stick in his mouth. This stick was for throwing, not smacking down misbehaving demons.

I checked the coast was clear before throwing the stick for him. I turned at the sound of a teeth jarring crack and saw Aurora slam a demon back down. For a witch who followed the white magic path, she sure looked thrilled to be pounding demons.

She wiped a hand across her forehead and grinned at me. "What's going on with these guys? They've got a bee in their twisted demon bonnets about something."

"Maybe they've stopped bitching at each other and decided it's better to work together to break out of our prison. Not that it will do them any good."

"Not when we're here with our fancy twirlers." Aurora spun the stick in her hand like a talented majorette.

I did the same, and the stick landed with a thud on the ground. "Whatever their plans are, we'll stop them."

"Over there! Here comes another one." Aurora pointed over my shoulder.

I raced in the direction of a red mist covering part of the cemetery.

"Tempest, this does not look good," Aurora whispered as she joined me, her fingers digging into my arm. "You know what a red mist means."

"That we won't get any freshly baked muffins from this demon," I said. Demons had different ways of emerging. Some appeared in a cloud of purple mist. Others favored green, but the ones you needed to worry about the most came with a red or black tinge. It promised twisted, nasty magic. Magic that burned your skin and threatened to send you mad if you spent any time immersed in it. That kind of evil was never permitted to run loose in our cemetery.

"We should call for backup," Aurora said. "Mom and Granny Dottie have more experience with this kind of demon."

The mist curled toward us as I raised my stick. "We don't need them. We've learned from the best."

Aurora adjusted the stick in her hand. "Are you sure?"

"Would your big sister ever lie to you?"

"You do about food."

I glanced at her out of the corner of my eye. "When have I ever lied about food?"

"At my eighth birthday party, when the chocolate cupcakes went missing. I knew you'd taken them, but you swore to Mom you hadn't."

"I don't remember that." Those cupcakes had been amazing. Rich and gooey and covered in popping candy. I'd eaten two every night for a week until they were too stale, sneaking the wrappers off and hiding under my covers as I read my book by torchlight. It was heaven.

"You do! I found the moldy wrappers under your bed."

I turned my full attention to Aurora. "You know better than to look under my bed."

Aurora huffed out a breath. "My friends thought I'd lied about those cupcakes."

"It didn't ruin the party. And you're still the most popular girl in Willow Tree Falls, even if you are too stingy to serve cupcakes at your birthday."

"Tempest!" Aurora glared at me. "Those were my party cupcakes."

I tapped my stick in my hand. "We can't focus on cupcakes. This demon smells like Baccaras. Do you remember him? I dragged him here after almost a month of searching. He stank so bad I had to burn my clothes."

Aurora sniffed the air and gagged. "Sulfur, rotten fish, and… what else is it?"

"I always thought he stank like used diapers."

"Yes! That's it. Baccaras smells of a soggy diaper." Aurora grinned at me. "We can handle him together."

Witches and demons were never close friends. There were a number of half-demons living in Willow Tree Falls, but the full-on demons were too chaotic to be trusted. They had lifetime bans unless they got a never-get-out-of-jail card from me.

Even though I hosted a particularly unpleasant demon, Frank, inside me in order to keep my sister safe, I had little time for them. When I wasn't in Willow Tree Falls, I was out capturing misbehaving demons and bringing them into Angel Force to deal with.

The ground trembled beneath our feet. It was a sure sign the demon was on his way.

We stood in an attack stance, sticks raised and knees bent, ready to swipe his head if he dared pop his horns out for a sniff of fresh air.

"Are you sure it's Baccaras?" Aurora whispered.

I shook my head. There were thousands of demons beneath our feet. I hadn't captured them all. Some had been here for hundreds of years, maybe longer. Monitoring the demon prison had been the family business for centuries. That's what the Crypt family did. We kept the rest of the world safe from devious demons.

The ground rumbled again, and a spurt of steam shot from a new crack.

"We should seal the crack before he comes through." Aurora stepped forward.

I grabbed her arm. "This demon needs to be taught a lesson. Try to escape our prison, and you end up with a bad headache and your power drained."

I glanced over my shoulder and was relieved to see Wiggles engrossed in chewing his stick. It was a habit he'd never had when he was a regular dog. Turn him into a hellhound and he developed a love of all things sticky. I didn't want Wiggles anywhere near a demon. Even though he was a hellhound and had a hide as tough as a rhino, they still might like to play with him.

My hand went to my stomach as Frank stirred. He'd been quiet these past three hours since I'd started working with Aurora, but I was taking a chance being around her for so long. Frank loved Aurora. Or rather, Frank would love to kill Aurora.

I stifled a sulfurous belch behind my hand as Frank's energy pulsed strongly. I took two steps away from Aurora. I didn't want her worrying about me when we had a demon trying to break free.

"Stay where you are," I muttered to Frank.

"Your charming sister is so close. I can smell her. What do you expect me to do?" His voice was just a whisper in my head.

"Slide out of me and head into the prison, like you're supposed to do." Frank was a stubborn son of a demon. All my attempts to get him out of me had failed. It seemed he liked living inside a witch.

"Where's the fun in that? If I was in there, I couldn't enjoy your fascinating company."

I snorted, and my fingers tightened around the stick. I'd get rid of Frank one day and finally be rid of his sweet tooth, bad attitude, and twisted desire to choke the life from my only sister.

"Here he comes," Aurora yelled as the red mist intensified and a low hissing emerged from the crack.

"Are you ready?" I asked her as the mist stung my eyes and blurred my vision.

She nodded, her blue eyes wide but a determined look on her face. "We've got this."

"It's time for a game of whack a demon." Wiggles trotted over.

"Don't get involved," I cautioned him. "You don't want to be dragged into the prison."

Wiggles cocked his head. "You'd come and get me if that happened."

"Sorry, buddy. You'd be on your own if you were dumb enough to get caught by a demon." I probably would get him out, but I wouldn't enjoy it.

Wiggles squinted up at me, his eyes glowing their usual hellhound red. "They'd love me down there. I'd fit right in."

I had to smile. He was right. Wiggles had a way of charming everybody, and now that he came with a nifty side order of hellhound, the demons wouldn't mind him at all. But Wiggles was my best friend, and no demon was getting its mean little claws on him.

I coughed as the mist grew thicker and swiped my hand across my face, so I wouldn't miss the moment the demon emerged.

"Do you see him?" Aurora yelled.

"I can barely see where you are," I said. "You?"

"Nothing yet. I'll get closer."

"Don't risk it," I yelled. "We'll know when he's here."

The ground bucked, and there was a ripping sound of stone grinding together as the crack grew larger.

I drew the stick over my head and inched closer. Any second now, the demon would poke his head out, and he'd be sorry when he did.

"Be careful of this one," Frank whispered in my head. "He likes to eat feisty witches for dinner."

"He can keep his demon paws off us," I muttered. "He's not getting to play tonight."

"Don't say I didn't warn you," Frank said.

That was an odd thing about Frank. Although his singular mission was to get free and attack Aurora, he came in handy now and again. His powers were wild and unpredictable, but when he gained control, there was little that could beat us. We were a weird and inappropriate double act.

I appreciated it when Frank's energy faded. Although he was a pain in the backside, he tended not to cause me much trouble when I needed to focus. I sometimes felt he was looking out for me, but that wasn't possible. Frank was chaos and evil. He was no-one's friendly uncle.

I grabbed a nearby headstone to stop from falling as the ground rumbled under my feet again.

"I think I see him," Aurora shouted. "Over here."

"Where's here?" I let go of the headstone and stumbled through the thick, sour smelling mist.

Aurora screamed, and I increased my pace, heading in the direction of the sound.

My eyes widened as I saw an enormous head, topped with black curling horns, jutting out of the crack in the ground. The crack had spread several yards across the cemetery, and Aurora stood at the opposite end to me, swiping her stick at the demon as his clawed arm flew through the air trying to reach her.

"No, you don't." I raced over and slammed my stick into the back of the demon's head repeatedly.

He roared but was unable to turn, given the tightness of the gap he was in. But he was inching his way out, and I did not want to see the rest of his enormous bulk come out of that crack.

Aurora joined the attack, and between us, we jabbed and poked, enraging him as he spat sharp shards of brimstone at us.

"It's working," Aurora yelled. "He's getting smaller. We're taking his energy."

I squinted at the demon. He was getting smaller, but he was also pulsing. That was a bad sign. "We should get back."

"We've almost got him," Aurora said. "A few more whacks, and he'll be back inside."

"I think he's going to—" the demon exploded in a hot shower of sticky red goo.

A huge backdraft sucked the majority of the goo toward me as the demon slid into the crack, muttering curses in Latin.

The gross smelling goo covered me from head to toe, and I was thrown off my feet as it slammed into my face. I landed on my back with a gasp and lay there staring up at the star-filled sky.

Wiggles trotted over and looked at me before shaking his head. "What is it with you and demon goo? You enjoy bathing in the stuff."

"Not out of choice." I swiped my hand over my goo covered mouth and grimaced. Demon goo always had the underlying taste of rotten eggs and sour milk.

I sat up slowly and shook goo off my favorite black jacket. I watched as Aurora expertly sealed the crack in the demon prison, and the last of the red mist evaporated, leaving nothing but a clear night lit by a large, pale moon.

As she walked over, I let out an exasperated sigh. Aurora had escaped all the demon goo. Her white pullover and fitted dark jeans were spotless. Other than a glow to her cheeks from the exercise we'd gotten smacking the demon, she looked like she'd just stepped out of a salon.

Aurora held her hand out to me. "It's time for a shift change."

I waved away her hand, not wanting to cover her in the sticky muck I'd just been showered in.

Aurora ignored me, grabbed my arm, and helped me to my feet. "I can get that jacket clean. It's just a bit of demon residue. You've been covered in worse."

I belched again, and Frank stirred, his interest more acute after Aurora had touched me. "Auntie Queenie should be here in a moment to take over."

Aurora nodded. She knew how tricky it was for us to spend too much time together without Frank crashing the party. She wisely dropped her hold on my arm and took a few steps back. "We did a great job tonight."

I smiled at her. "We make a good team."

"Did someone say tea?" Auntie Queenie strolled over, a large bag slung over one arm and a pastry in her free hand.

Aurora hurried over and kissed her cheek. "We were saying it was almost time for you to get here."

"I'm here, right on time." She looked around the cemetery. "It seems quiet." Her gaze went to the goo splattered on me and the ground, but she didn't pass comment.

I exchanged a smile with Aurora. "We've been bored all night. Nothing to do but play cards and count stars."

Auntie Queenie sidestepped the goo as she finished her pastry. "Tempest, you get off and see how Cloven Hoof is doing. We can handle things from here."

I nodded goodbye and hurried out of the cemetery with Wiggles. My bar, Cloven Hoof, sat at the other end of Willow Tree Falls, only a ten-minute walk from the cemetery. It was a specialist bar, serving mildly magical and completely legal treats. Other than when we had the occasional party, it was a chilled-out place, and it was just where I wanted to be tonight. Hunting demons was stressful.

I headed to the front door and nodded at Suki, who stood outside.

Suki was a new recruit to Cloven Hoof. Being a giant wood nymph with muscular arms like gnarled tree trunks, she did an excellent job as an intimidating bouncer.

"How's everything going tonight?" I asked her.

Her gaze traveled over my goo splattered appearance before she nodded. "There are plenty of people in, but they're behaving themselves."

"Tempest Crypt, as I live and breathe."

I turned and stared at the three guys approaching Cloven Hoof. I groaned inwardly as I recognized Dewey Lavern, Puddle Lavern's nephew. He'd always been a smarmy git when growing up. Now that he was an adult, nothing had changed.

"Dewey, what brings you to Willow Tree Falls?" I asked him. "The last time I saw you here, you said this village was too backward for your city tastes."

"Visiting my auntie. Mom said the old girl gets lonely living in that cottage on her own." He smirked and shoved his thick, dark hair off his forehead. Some people might consider Dewey attractive, but his eyes always looked cold to me. "That's an interesting look you're wearing." His gaze ran over my ruined clothing.

I flicked goo off my hand, so it splattered on the ground by his feet. "I'm trying something new."

Dewey kicked dirt over the goo. "These are my friends, Serath Duckle and Bart Ranger. We're staying a few days. I'm showing them around my childhood home."

I nodded at the two guys with him. I'd seen them with Dewey before on his rare visits. Serath was tall and pale with large blue eyes. Bart was shorter and stockier with a stubbled chin and dark eyes that swept around as if he was looking for something.

"Even with gross goo on you, you're looking good, Tempest," Dewey said. "Are you still single?"

"As ever, just as I like it."

"We'll come to Cloven Hoof later. You can buy me a drink, and we can catch up."

"Tempest doesn't need to buy the drinks in here, buddy," Wiggles said. "She owns the place."

Dewey stared at Wiggles. "It talks."

"Well spotted." I nudged Wiggles with my calf as he growled. "Cloven Hoof might not be the place for you. You should try the Ancient Imp."

"That's where we're going now. I'll look in later when the place gets livelier."

"This is as lively as it gets. I like it that way." I shook my head as I watched them saunter away, a picture of cocky arrogance. There was no room for idiots in my life and definitely no room for Dewey Lavern and his dodgy friends.

"That guy is a jerk," Wiggles said.

I nodded. "You always were an excellent judge of character."

"I bet he's not had a date in years. He stinks of desperate loser."

"Does not dating make you a loser?"

"Absolutely." He tilted his head to look at me. "It's why I keep telling you to marry Brogan."

Suki coughed into her hand, and I saw a smile on her face as she looked away.

"Brogan Costin is part vampire."

"So?"

"So, he might like a plump little hellhound to nibble on at night. If we start dating, he could mistake you as a snack."

"Who are you calling plump?"

I laughed. "You don't mind being a vampire snack, but you mind me pointing out your pot belly?"

"I do not have a pot belly. Besides, I bite back. If Brogan decided I'd make a good hot dog, I'd soon change his mind." He gnashed his teeth together.

"Come on," I said to Wiggles. "Less talk about marrying me off. I need to get rid of this demon goo."

"Then we can have cake."

"Only if you want a bigger belly. I was thinking we can do some work behind the bar. And I've got a stack of paperwork to go through."

"But first cake," Wiggles said. "And no more talking about my belly, or I'll get a complex."

I grinned as I opened the door to Cloven Hoof and let Wiggles in. He might have a little belly, but I adored it. I did not adore him trying to hook me up with Brogan, although Brogan did make the best breakfasts in the whole of Willow Tree Falls.

I had enough on my plate without dating. Paperwork beckoned, and it seemed, so did cake if Wiggles had anything to do with it.

That's what occupied my time. Demons, paperwork, goo, and the occasional cake. That was fine by me.

Chapter 2

There was a lovely chilled vibe in the bar as I wandered around. I'd taken a shower, found some cake to keep Wiggles happy, and was settled in a seat at the bar as I watched my two new bar staff, Ginger Gibson and Blaze Dubrovnik, serve customers.

They'd only been here a few weeks but fit right in. They were new to Willow Tree Falls. Ginger was a Green witch, gaining her powers from Mother Nature. Blaze was a mixture of warlock and human and had a handy fire trick he used to entertain the staff.

Business was good, profits were up, and the new staff meant everyone got to take time off and not get over-worked and think about quitting.

Merrie Noble walked over and placed a lemon drop in front of me, alongside a bowl of dried mushrooms. "These are our freshest batch. I thought the boss might like to taste test the produce and give it her seal of approval."

I dipped my finger into the bowl and sampled a mushroom. It fizzed lightly on my tongue as the magic slid through me. "Perfection."

Merrie grinned. "We aim to please."

Merrie was an amazing bar manager. I could rely on her to ensure Cloven Hoof ran smoothly. I never worried when I had to leave on my demon hunting duties.

I gave a contented sigh as I downed my lemon drop. I loved Cloven Hoof when it was like this, lots of happy, chilled-out customers. Music played in the background, but it wasn't overwhelming, so people could have a decent conversation without yelling. Equally, they could slide into a booth at the back of the bar, relax, and not be bothered by anybody.

This had always been my plan with Cloven Hoof, create a chilled place where people could come and forget their worries.

The sound of raucous laughter had me turning in my seat. I groaned when I spotted Dewey, Serath, and Bart walk through the doorway. They looked like they'd enjoyed themselves a little too much at the Ancient Imp. Serath appeared unsteady on his feet as they headed to the bar, and Bart and Dewey leaned on each other for support.

"Are they friends of yours?" Merrie asked.

"I wouldn't call them friends. The tall one with the overly styled hair is Puddles' nephew. He's visiting for a couple of days."

Merrie nodded. "He's been here before. Do you want me to keep an eye on them?"

"Sure, I'll do the same. It looks like they're not here for a relaxing time. We don't want them scaring away the other customers." I watched them as they reached the bar.

Izzie Argan, another member of my bar staff, was unfortunate enough to serve them. Her smile faded, and a tightness appeared around her eyes as they spoke to her.

"It looks like they're off to a bad start." I stood from my seat, but Merrie waved me back down.

"Stay there. I've got this. You've had enough idiots to deal with for one night after working a shift in the cemetery."

I sat back down, but my attention remained on the group. Merrie waved Izzie away and quickly served the three guys.

Whatever they'd said to Izzie, she was not happy. She was speaking to Ginger and scowling at them from the end of the bar, her sunny disposition gone and deep frown lines lacing either side of her mouth. Her behavior was unusual. Izzie handled difficult customers easily, even when they got excited, but the way she glared at this group made me think they'd said something inappropriate.

The guys downed their drinks and ordered more. They might be good for business, but I'd rather have less money and fewer troublemakers.

The door to the bar opened. Suki poked her head through. She looked at me and nodded at Dewey and his friends.

Now, there was a good idea. Suki was sweet-natured, but rile her, and she turned into a lethal, unstoppable fighting machine. She could even knock an angel on its feathery butt when she had a mind to do so.

I nodded at the group. It was time for Dewey and his friends to calm down or take a hike.

Suki strode in, her hands fisted as she approached the group.

I watched in amusement as they turned and all stared up at Suki, their mouths open.

Whatever she said to them worked. They grabbed their drinks and left the bar, scurrying to a booth at the back.

I nodded thanks to her, and she shrugged before heading back outside. Suki had been one of the best hires I'd ever made for Cloven Hoof. She fit right in, and her size and intimidating presence meant trouble stopped before it even started. Nobody wanted to be on the wrong end of Suki's fists.

Even though the group had disappeared and stopped bothering my bar staff, I'd still keep an eye on those three idiots. They were not going to ruin everybody's night.

"Hey, Tempest." Axel Shadowsoul strode over, dressed in a tailored gray suit and open-necked white shirt.

As a half-demon, Axel came with a nifty set of skills and a side order of serious smooth, which sometimes slid into sleazy. He was always well turned out and charming and often directed that charm at me.

"I hope you're not here to buy any produce." Axel had a small addiction issue when it came to my mushrooms. He'd been off them for months and was doing well, but the temptation would always be there.

"I'm being a good boy, as always. I'm here for a drink and to soak up some fun. You've got a good crowd in tonight." He settled on the stool next to me and ordered a drink for us both.

I nodded as I looked around the bar. "I've no complaints."

"Your new barmaid is cute," Axel said. "I love the red hair."

Axel was always looking for a new conquest. It was why I never took his interest in me seriously. I was fond of him, but it was more like a fondness you have for an annoying big brother. Even though he tried to convince me otherwise, Axel was a player. He always would be.

"That's Ginger. Be careful of her. She's got a great connection with Mother Nature. You mess with her, and you'll find your home attacked by angry giant triffids."

"Sounds interesting."

"No, direct that interest elsewhere. She's great at her job, so don't go messing around with her."

Axel's smile turned sly. "Would you like me to direct my interest at you?"

I shook my head. "No, thanks."

Axel raised a hand and pressed it to his heart. "I never mess around with gorgeous women. You should know that." He winked at me as the drinks arrived.

I turned at the sound of raised voices. Dewey stood by a booth, glowering at Serath and Bart.

"What's with that lot?" Axel asked.

"They're three enormous pains in my backside," I said. "I should have kicked them out as soon as they came in."

"I know that one," Axel said. "Isn't that Puddles' Lavern's nephew?"

"That's right," I said, "and his two idiot friends."

"Calm down, man," Serath said. "I didn't mean anything."

"You're a jerk." Dewey lunged at Serath and grabbed him in a messy headlock.

I jumped off my seat and raced over. Fighting was not allowed in Cloven Hoof.

Axel ran alongside me. "Need a hand?"

"It's okay. I've got this."

"I will never let a woman go into a fight on her own, even if she does have your incredible skills."

I shrugged. It was up to Axel if he wanted to risk his own neck.

"Hey, that's enough!" I grabbed Dewey by the shoulder and pulled him off Serath.

Dewey turned and shoved me away, fury coloring his cheeks scarlet. "Keep out of this. It's not your business."

"That's where you're wrong. This is my business. You're standing in my business. You all need to leave."

Bart jumped up and joined Dewey and Serath. "We're having a bit of fun, Tempest. No harm done."

"Go have your fun elsewhere."

"You're throwing us out?" Dewey grinned and nudged Bart.

"Yes. All three of you are out of here." I gestured at the door.

"No, we're staying," Dewey said. "Tempest, chill out. We're old friends."

"No, we're not. Get out of here."

Dewey and Bart shared a sharp look.

"What are you going to do about it?" Bart asked.

"He did not just say that," Axel muttered.

"Yeah, little witch," Dewey said. "You're not so tough now there are three of us." He glanced at Serath. "Are you in or still wanting to bitch at me?"

Serath shrugged and moved to stand next to Dewey, not meeting my gaze.

Oh, this would be fun. "It's time you all left. You're not welcome here."

"You're banning us," Dewey sneered. "Like you could stop us from coming in."

"You'd be surprised what Tempest can do," Axel said as he squared up to Dewey.

I placed a hand on his arm to stop him from getting involved. "I don't want trouble. You've all had enough for one night. Why don't you go to your aunt's and sleep it off?"

"Why don't you come with us?" Dewey jabbed me on the shoulder. "We could have quite a party, the four of us."

"You couldn't handle me," I said. "And I don't associate with morons."

"You're hanging out with this guy." Dewey pointed at Axel.

"I make an exception for Axel."

Axel glowered at Dewey. "Can I punch him yet?" he asked me.

"No punching. These three are going to walk calmly out of the bar."

"No, I don't think we are." Dewey whacked Axel around the head. It was a clumsy punch and showed he had more skills at talking tough than acting it.

"Suki!" I yelled as I dodged Dewey's fist and jumped backward.

Axel was doubled over by the booth. Dewey's punch was more effective than I'd realized. Bart jumped on Axel's back and pummeled him.

Dewey turned his attention to me and gestured at Serath. "Come on. Let's take this smug witch down a peg or two."

Frank stirred inside me as the tension grew. I pushed against him. I didn't want him emerging inside Cloven Hoof. Whenever he made an appearance, Frank always left behind a heap of expensive damage.

The floor shuddered beneath my feet. Suki flew past me and sucker-punched Serath and Dewey at the same time.

They flew backward and hit the ground.

She stood over them, her face a picture of fury. "You do not harm Tempest."

They lay there, staring at her, dazed expressions on their faces.

"Thanks, Suki. Get these idiots out of here." I patted her arm.

I glanced over to see Axel still struggling with Bart. I dashed over and yanked Bart off his back. "You too. The only person who gets to mess with Axel's pretty face is me."

Bart staggered backward. He made a move toward me, but Suki's hand wrapping around his throat made him pause. He glared up at her and then raised his hands in submission. "Fine, I'll go."

With Suki's help, we herded the three of them out the door and slammed it shut behind them.

"Is everything okay, boss?" Suki asked. "They didn't hurt you?"

"I'm fine. Everything is fine, thanks to you and your incredible fists."

She ducked her head and blushed. "That's what I'm here for. I'll head outside and make sure they don't come back."

I turned to see everyone in the bar watching us. "The show is over, folks. Business as usual."

Axel staggered over, groaning as he did so. "I almost had that guy. I just needed to get his hand off my throat and he'd have been history."

I shook my head as I patted his shoulder. "You're my hero."

His smile was rueful. "More like Suki is our hero. That wood nymph has some moves."

"That's why she's here." I let out a sigh and leaned against the wall, my pulse racing from the fight. So much for a quiet night. I'd trust my instinct the next time I encountered Dewey and his buddies. Steer clear. Their money was not worth my trouble.

Chapter 3

I rolled over and my nose bumped Wiggles' tummy as he lay sprawled next to me on the bed.

I groaned as I heard the incessant whirring of my snow globe in the lounge, alerting me to an incoming message.

"It's too early," I grumbled as I stuffed my pillow over my head.

"Biting the dark handsome parts." Wiggles sounded like he was having an interesting dream.

"I'll bite whoever is calling me this early in the morning." I let out a sigh as the noise stopped. It began again a few seconds later.

I rolled out of bed, stuffed my feet into my slippers, and stomped into the living room. I grabbed the snow globe and shook it to activate the call.

"Oh, Tempest! I'm so glad you're there." Puddles Lavern's pastel blue hair filled most of the image.

"Are you calling to say I'm being evicted?"

"By the witch's hat! Of course not."

"Has there been a family emergency?"

"Well, now that you mention it. My—"

"I meant my family."

"Oh! Of course. Well, I hope not."

"So, what's the problem?" Puddles was a realtor who ran Gnome Place Like Home. She was also my landlady, something she reminded me of if I was ever overdue on the rent for the apartment.

"I know I'm going to sound like an overprotective auntie, but I'm hunting for my boys."

"Your boys?" I rubbed my eyes. Was this some kind of terrible nightmare?

"Yes, Dewey said he was taking his friends to Cloven Hoof last night. I was hoping you'd seen them. They're such good boys, and I thought they deserved a night out to enjoy themselves. I told them to be back by eleven, though. Growing boys need their sleep."

I muttered several rude words under my breath. Dewey and his idiot friends were more than capable of looking after themselves. "I saw them."

"That's such a relief. I was getting worried. You see, they didn't come home last night."

I grunted. "And you think I have something to do with that?"

"Oh, no. But I'd hoped you'd seen them."

"They were at Cloven Hoof. They caused my customers trouble, so I got them to leave."

"My Dewey can be a little boisterous. He's been so looking forward to his visit. They had to delay their arrival by several weeks, so they'll all be excited." Puddles giggled. "I expect Dewey was showing off for his friends."

"Most likely."

"He's truly a good boy. It was high spirits. I expect he'll be around first thing this morning to apologize."

I shuddered, doubting that very much. "Is Dewey in trouble?"

"No, not that I know of." Puddles' face grew closer to the globe. "Do you think he's in trouble?"

"No, but I wanted to know why you're chasing him."

"Oh! Well, I'm worried."

"Puddles, he's a grown man. He most likely found some company to enjoy last night."

Puddles tutted. "Not my Dewey. He's an upstanding young man. He wouldn't go off with some floozy who caught his eye."

I resisted the urge to laugh. If he got the chance, he would. I'd watched him sleazing over several women in the bar, including my bar staff. "Well, then he must be having a sleepover somewhere else. You don't need to worry. There was nothing wrong with him when he was evicted from Cloven Hoof."

"You evicted him! What for?"

"That's a conversation to have with your nephew. Now, if you'll excuse me, I have a comfy bed to get back to." I shook the snow globe and dismissed Puddles.

"Talk about an overprotective aunt." I stomped back to my bed and flung myself on it. With a bit of luck, I would return to the lovely dream I was having that involved melted chocolate, some toasted cheese sandwiches, and a huge tub of triple chocolate ice cream.

"Tempest, wake up!"

My eyes snapped open. I jerked upright and grabbed a pillow to protect myself. I blinked and stared into Puddles' big blue eyes. "What are you doing in my apartment?"

She shrugged and looked at the key in her hand. "As your landlady, I have a right to a spare key."

I glowered at her. "You don't have the right to barge in whenever you like."

"It's an emergency. I had no choice."

"If the building is burning down, that's the only emergency I care about."

Wiggles opened one eye and stared at Puddles. "Am I dreaming?"

"Sadly not," I said.

He rolled off the bed and broke wind. The room filled with the unpleasant scent of brimstone. It was an unfortunate side effect of being a hellhound. He trotted around the bed and sat in front of Puddles, giving his belly a thorough scratch with a back foot. "Have you brought us breakfast?"

Puddles took a step back and wafted a hand in front of her face. "No, I'm here about my nephew."

Wiggles glanced at me and shook his head before wandering out of the bedroom.

"I already told you I saw Dewey and his friends last night. They caused a scene at Cloven Hoof, so they had to leave. That's all I can tell you." I lowered the pillow back on the bed.

Puddles clasped her hands in front of her. "I'm so worried about him. Dewey always comes home. This is so unlike him."

I gritted my teeth and thought calming thoughts. "I'm sure it's nothing. And it's certainly not a good reason for you to come here and wake me up."

Puddles looked a little shamefaced. "I want to make sure he's okay. My sister is so protective of Dewey. She rarely lets him out of her sight. That's why he visits so infrequently."

Knowing what a selfish little toad Dewey was, that was most likely not true, but I didn't want to burst Puddles' happy bubble. I sighed and rolled out of bed, tempted to follow Wiggles' routine of scratching and breaking wind, but I resisted the urge.

"Let's go to the kitchen, and I'll make coffee."

"I have no time for coffee," Puddles said. "I just want to know where Dewey is."

I rolled my shoulders as I walked into the kitchen. "I do. I barely function at this time of the day without caffeine."

"He wasn't acting strangely last night when you saw him?" Puddles asked as she paced my living room. "I was worried he might have gotten sick when he was out and fell into a ditch."

"Fell into a ditch?"

"You hear all kinds of horrible stories. Do you remember about ten years ago that visitor who wandered into the swamp? They never did find him."

"That was a rumor. I bet he simply left Willow Tree Falls. Not everyone loves village life. You know, people knowing all your business and where you live, that sort of thing."

Puddles raised her chin, a stubborn look on her face. "It could have happened."

"Dewey probably had too much to drink and is sleeping it off somewhere. He'll roll in in a few hours, all apologetic, and you can forgive him." I gestured to the coffee pot, but Puddles shook her head.

"I'm sure you were overreacting when you threw him out of Cloven Hoof. Maybe that's when he fell in the ditch," Puddles said.

"Dewey attacked Axel. We had to throw him and his friends out for starting a fight."

"I don't understand. Dewey must be unwell to behave like that," Puddles murmured.

"He seemed quite happy to play the role of fist swinging oaf."

Puddles' eyes narrowed. "You said *we* had to throw them out. Who else was involved?"

"Suki. My bouncer."

"Oh! She's very large, and I hear she has a temper. You don't think she did anything nasty to Dewey, do you?"

"I'm sure she didn't. We threw them out, and that was it."

"I'd better talk to Suki," Puddles said. "She might have seen something suspicious."

"That's a terrible idea."

Puddles' eyes widened. "Why? Is she dangerous?"

"I expect so if you wake her up like you just did me."

Puddles' hand fluttered against her chest before she nodded. "I insist. This is important. Where is she?"

I tipped my head back and groaned. When Puddles wanted something, she hung onto it like an angry terrier. "Here's the deal. You make the coffee, and I'll go get Suki. She also likes coffee. She will need coffee to cope with you flapping around her."

Puddles nodded. "Very well."

I stumbled down the stairs and past the bar. The whole place felt asleep, just like I wanted to be.

I flicked on the lights in the cellar and crept down the wooden steps. After Suki had started working here, she'd asked if she could use the cellar as a place to sleep. She had her own home in the forest, but after a visiting journalist was murdered close to where she lived, she no longer felt safe there. I was more than happy to offer her a bed, and she'd insisted the cellar was ideal.

I paused at the bottom step and could hear Suki's deep breathing. She had a single bed in the corner, piled high with covers and throws. It looked cozy. I'd said she could sleep in the bar where it was warmer, but she was used to sleeping somewhere cool, having spent most of her life in the forest.

I tiptoed over and nudged her arm. "Suki, please don't kill me."

She groaned and rolled onto her back, blinking sleep out of her eyes. "Is everything okay?"

"Everything is fine. We have a panicking Puddles Lavern upstairs. She's not leaving until she talks to you."

"About what?" Suki yawned loudly and stretched her arms over her head.

"Her moron nephew and his friends. Any chance you can help?"

Suki's expression was puzzled as she slid from her bed and pushed her feet into a pair of gray fluffy slippers with unicorn horns on the big toes. "Sure. What does she need to know about her nephew?"

"She's panicking because he didn't come home last night."

Suki rubbed her forehead. "They caused a lot of trouble."

"You don't need to remind me of that. Puddles wears rose-tinted glasses when it comes to her nephew." We walked up the cellar steps and were met at the top by Puddles.

"I thought you were making coffee," I said to her.

"I did. It's on the bar." She pointed to two mugs.

I hurried to the mugs and passed one to Suki, who stumbled past Puddles with a cautious look on her face.

"What did you see after you unnecessarily threw my nephew and his friends out of the bar?" Puddles asked Suki.

Suki took a long drink of coffee, her gaze on me.

"It's fine. Tell her everything. It might make her panic less."

Puddles glared at me. "I'm not panicking. I'm worried as all good aunties should be when a beloved relative vanishes."

Suki set down her mug. "There wasn't much to see. The tall, blond one started arguing with the other two."

"That would be Serath," Puddles said. "What did they argue about?"

"I don't know. They were too far away to hear. Serath shoved the chubby dark guy and the other one with the lovely hair. Is that your nephew?"

Puddles nodded. "He has such thick hair. It makes him even more handsome."

Suki glanced at me and shrugged. "Sure. Bart had to pull Serath and Dewey apart. After that, Serath stormed off alone, and the other two walked in the opposite direction without him."

"Oh dear, that doesn't sound good," Puddles said.

"I'm sure it was high spirits and too much drink," I said. "You should check at the Ancient Imp to see if they went there. It looked like they weren't finished for the night."

"I've been there. Petra saw them earlier in the evening. You're the last people to see them."

"Give them a few hours to wake up from wherever they're sleeping it off, and you can ask them yourself what happened," I said. "They'll come skulking in soon enough with bad heads. I'd bet money on it."

Puddles worried her bottom lip with her teeth, chewing off her pink gloss. "I need to report this to Angel Force."

I blinked at her in surprise. "What are you going to report? Three grown men go out for a night and don't tell their auntie where they're going?"

"You wouldn't understand. You're not an auntie."

"It's not that hard to figure out," I said. "Angel Force won't be interested."

"It's the right thing to do, especially since they were fighting. You know what these young men get like."

"They get rude and inappropriate," I said, "as I witnessed here last night."

Puddles frowned at me. "You'll feel bad when they're all found in a ditch." She turned and hurried out of the bar.

I shook my head. What was Puddles' obsession with ditches?

Suki leaned against the bar as she finished her coffee. "What does Puddles think happened?"

I sipped my own coffee and rubbed my forehead. "She's overreacting, but she won't leave us alone until they're found. If the angels won't help, Puddles will keep hassling us."

"I can help you look for them." Suki yawned and rubbed her eyes again.

"No, you get back to bed. You had a late night, just like I did."

Suki nodded. "Thanks. I could do with a few more hours." She downed the last of her coffee and headed back to the cellar.

I grabbed my mug and walked up to the apartment. After a quick shower and a change of clothes, I was out of Cloven Hoof with Wiggles by my side. It was rare for me to be up so early, and the morning was chilly. I was glad of my extra layers and the black and white scarf with panda faces on it that Aurora had given me as a birthday present.

"Are we really hunting those drunken idiots?" Wiggles asked as he trotted beside me.

"Yep, and we'll keep hunting so long as it gets Puddles off our back. I do not ever want to be woken again to find her staring at me." I shuddered. "And I'm going to have words with her about using that spare key."

"You should change the locks."

"That's not a bad idea." I shrugged. "Although, she'd use magic to bust her way in if she was desperate enough."

I grabbed two breakfast muffins to go from Sprinkles and headed to the cemetery as we ate them. There was always at least one member of my family on shift. Maybe they'd seen something late last night after I chucked Dewey and his gang out of Cloven Hoof.

Granny Dottie poked her head out of an open crypt as I walked around the graves, hunting for family members.

She gave a cheery wave. "I didn't know you were taking a shift today."

"I'm not. I was rudely awoken by Puddles looking for her missing nephew and his friends. I don't suppose they dropped by here last night, did they?"

"Missing friends. What a thing." Granny Dottie hurried out of the crypt, sporting an enormous purple scarf wrapped around her throat. "Why would they come here?"

"It's quiet and has plenty of places to lie down. You didn't see them, did you?"

Granny Dottie tugged on the end of her scarf and shuffled her feet. "Well, it's funny you should say that."

My eyes widened. "Hold on. Have you seen them?"

She crossed her arms over her chest. "I couldn't leave the poor boys out here. They wandered into the cemetery, joking about seeing ghosts and scaring each other. They sat down near a recently sealed crack. I didn't want a demon to leap out and grab them, even though they were being boisterous."

"What did you do with them?"

Granny Dottie shrugged and glanced over her shoulder. "Come this way." She led me back into the crypt.

Dewey and Bart were curled on their sides with blankets over them.

I stared at the sleeping guys. "Puddles will have a fit when she realizes you've been keeping her precious nephew inside a crypt."

"It's a lot safer than being out in the cemetery. We had three more cracks open last night. I barely had a chance to get any reading done, and I've got a particularly steamy novel on the go. I'm picking up a few tips to keep your grandpa keen."

I grimaced and wiped those words from my memory. I leaned over Dewey and Bart, and my heart sped up. They had blood on their knuckles.

I looked around. "We're missing one. Where's Serath?"

"Only two came in last night. They did mention a Serath, but they were both so merry I could barely make sense of what they were saying. I tucked them in this crypt and let them sleep it off."

"Do you see the marks on their knuckles? They fought in Cloven Hoof last night, but I don't think they got those marks then."

Granny Dottie inspected their hands. "They do look a little worse for wear, poor things."

"They're not poor things. They're drunken idiots who messed up a perfectly decent night at Cloven Hoof." I nudged them with my foot.

After several increasingly hard nudges, Dewey and Bart both groaned and stirred to life.

"Wake up!"

They blinked up at me in surprise.

"Where am I?" Dewey asked.

"In our cemetery," I said. "And you're a wanted man."

Dewey eased himself upright and pinched the bridge of his nose. "I feel terrible."

"You look worse," I said.

He peered up at me. "What am I wanted for?"

"Your auntie is on the war path. She thinks something bad happened to you because you didn't come home last night. She woke me to tell me that exciting bit of news."

Dewey groaned. "Auntie Puddles is so protective."

Bart looked around and yawned loudly. "I don't remember coming here."

"You were both rather tipsy last night," Granny Dottie said cheerfully. "I thought you might like a little sleep inside one of our crypts. It's safer here. Less chance of being eaten."

Dewey stared at her. "Oh, I remember. Did you roll me in here?"

Granny Dottie chuckled. "You needed help walking. It was good fun. I rolled you around for a while."

"Where's Serath?" I asked Dewey.

Dewey and Bart looked around as if expecting to find him hiding in a corner.

"No clue," Dewey finally said.

"Suki saw you arguing with him after you left Cloven Hoof. What did you argue about?"

Dewey scrubbed a hand down his face. "I don't remember us arguing."

"Look at your fists. You argued with someone."

Dewey blinked at his bloody knuckles. "I guess I did. I don't think it was Serath."

I shook my head. They were worse than useless. "Time to get out of our cemetery. You need to show me where you went after your fight with Serath. He might be lying in a ditch somewhere." I smirked to myself. I was getting as bad as Puddles.

"Didn't we go to the forest?" Dewey asked Bart. "I sort of remember being surrounded by lots of trees and mossy crud."

"That's right," Bart said.

"Why would you go there late at night?"

"For fun," Dewey said. "Since you chucked us out of Cloven Hoof, we were all out of options."

"You could have gone to bed."

"Nah. That would have been boring."

I nudged him with the toe of my boot again. "Get up. Show me where you went. Maybe we'll find Serath asleep." As much as I didn't want to be involved, I also didn't want Cloven Hoof getting a bad reputation for letting in trouble makers. And I didn't want the rumor getting around that people who visited Cloven Hoof went missing afterwards.

After several pathetic attempts and a lot of complaining, Dewey and Bart were on their feet.

I said goodbye to Granny Dottie and herded them out of the cemetery and toward the forest.

"Can we get coffee?" Dewey pleaded. "I feel awful."

"You can have coffee after we find your friend," I said.

They both grumbled under their breaths as I marched them to the edge of the forest.

"Which path did you take?" I asked.

They looked around as if it was the first time they'd ever seen trees.

"It all looks the same," Dewey said.

"I think we went that way." Bart pointed a limp hand to the left.

We wandered slowly around the forest, Wiggles happy to run around and snuffle in all kinds of disgusting things.

My mood grew increasingly dark as it became clear neither Dewey nor Bart had a clue where they were last night.

"Tempest!"

I turned to see Rhett Blackthorn. He was his usual gorgeous fallen angel self, decked out in black and his dark hair swept off his face.

He smiled at me, and I ignored the fluttering feeling in my stomach. "What brings you into the forest so early?"

"We're hunting for idiots. What about you?" I was surprised to see him here. Rhett was not a morning person.

He looked at Dewey and Bart. "The same."

My eyes narrowed. Rhett was full of secrets. He must be doing something dodgy if he was up with the sun.

"I don't suppose you've seen anyone sleeping off a heavy night in the forest? A tall, blond guy," I asked him.

"I've not come across anybody, but I've only been here a few minutes."

I nodded as I kept an eye on Dewey and Bart to make sure they didn't scarper to the cafe for their coffee.

"What's this guy done wrong to have you on his tail?"

"Gotten lost." I shrugged. "It's nothing, but we'd better find him before the werewolves do."

"Werewolves!" Bart looked at me and staggered backward. "There aren't werewolves here."

"Of course not." Dewey shot me a dirty look.

There were, but they were mostly harmless, old, and had very few teeth. Still, they were a great deterrent to stop drunken fools poking around where they didn't need to be poking.

"I can help you look if you'd like," Rhett said.

"Tempest!" Wiggles bounded through the trees. "I found something."

"Is it a big stick?"

"It's nothing that fun."

"A pile of yeti poop?"

"Yuck! I do not touch the hard stuff." Wiggles bounced on his paws. "It's nasty. You'll love it."

"Okay, let's take a look." I was getting nowhere trailing around with Dewey and Bart.

Wiggles glanced at Rhett. "You're drooling. Tempest doesn't look that hot first thing in the morning." He turned and raced away before I could yell at him.

I hurried after Wiggles and Rhett joined me. "Don't mind Wiggles. He's always rude when he's hungry."

Rhett chuckled. "He must get hungry a lot."

"That hellhound is always starving."

We followed behind Wiggles and entered a small clearing close to the swamp.

"What is it?" I asked Wiggles.

"I'm no police dog, but I've picked up the smell of blood. And it looks like there's been a fight."

I looked around the clearing. There were scuff marks on the ground as if people had been running around and dragging things. "Dewey, Bart, get over here," I yelled.

They wandered over, looking miserable, pale and grumpy.

"Does this place look familiar?"

They both looked around and shook their heads.

"It all looks the same to me," Dewey said. "It might look better after I've had breakfast. Your treat."

"Wiggles is right." Rhett examined the ground. "There's blood here."

"Blood!" Dewey said. "Is it a wounded animal?"

Rhett shrugged. "It's hard to say. This doesn't look good. There's a lot of blood."

I glared at Dewey and Bart. "Are you sure there's nothing you want to tell me about what happened here last night? You didn't have a fight with Serath and it got out of hand?"

"No!" Bart said.

Dewey nudged him. "It wasn't a fight exactly."

"You did hit Serath?" I glanced at Dewey's puffy knuckles.

"We had a disagreement. It was nothing bad. I don't think blood was spilled."

"You and Serath met again after your argument outside Cloven Hoof?"

"Oh! Yes, we did. I remember." Bart rubbed the end of his nose. "He charged after us and tackled Dewey to the ground."

"He did not! I dodged him."

Bart laughed. "You both hit the ground hard. It was hilarious."

"The only hilarious thing around here is you," Dewey muttered.

"How bad was the fight?" I asked.

Dewey raised his hands. "It was nothing. We had a few angry words, swung a few punches, and Serath flounced off. He's lousy in a fight. He gets all girly and squeals. No offense, Tempest."

"Offense taken." I looked around and sighed. "I'd better alert Angel Force. If something bad went down, they'll need to know." I used my mobile snow globe to send a message to Dazielle.

I was tempted to scarper, knowing how officious Angel Force got with anything like this, but they'd only come after me later if I disappeared.

Whatever happened here, it was not good. I had a bad feeling Dewey and Bart had done something horrible to their missing friend.

Chapter 4

It took less than ten minutes before three angels descended from the sky.

Dazielle hurried over, her outfit its usual pristine white and her long, blonde hair gleaming. "Have you touched any of the evidence?"

"Good morning to you," I said. "Wiggles has bounced around the scene a few times, but other than that, we've kept our distance."

Dazielle introduced herself to Dewey and Bart before standing and staring at the clearing with her hands on her hips. "We need to get this area clear, so you don't tamper with the evidence."

"Of a crime that might not have been committed," I said.

"You're not the expert here," Dazielle said. "Stand back while we see what we're dealing with."

I was happy to get out of their way and waited with Dewey and Bart while the angels did their work.

"You'd better not be hiding anything," I said to them quietly. "The angels will question you about where Serath is. If your fight was serious, come clean. He could be lying somewhere, badly injured."

Dewey shot me a sly look. "Nothing bad happened."

"You argued at Cloven Hoof. What was that about?"

"A cute bit of skirt. Serath was interested in one of your bar staff. We knew he had no chance. We yanked his chain about it, and he took offense. He is lousy at taking a joke."

"You were fighting over a woman?"

"It's true," Bart said. "Serath has the worst luck with girls. He has an eye for the ones who enjoy turning him down."

Dewey nodded. "You'd think he was cursed, the way they reject him. He's a total failure when it comes to finding a girlfriend."

"And you continued that fight after you left Cloven Hoof?" I glanced at the angels who were busy doing I wasn't sure what, but it gave me time to grill Dewey and Bart.

"Serath carried on the fight. He must have doubled back and followed us into the woods. Bart was telling the truth. I got jumped and defended myself," Dewey said.

"Why use your fists?" I asked. "You're both magic users."

Dewey shrugged and scuffed a foot along the ground. "I'm not all that good when it comes to magic."

Bart chuckled. "You're lousy at magic. Even a basic spell backfires."

"Shut it," Dewey muttered. "You're no better. You'd make a simple wart spell go wrong because you never concentrate."

"My boys! My boys!" Puddles raced through the forest, her blue hair puffing out around her ruddy cheeks.

Dewey grimaced and forced a smile. "Auntie Puddles."

She flung her arms around him. "I've been so worried about you. When I heard Angel Force had come into the forest, I panicked and thought that something bad had happened to you."

"Nothing bad has happened to him," I said. "But Serath is missing."

Puddles continued to cling to Dewey as he struggled to get out of her embrace. "I'm sure Serath is fine. I'm just happy to have my Dewey back."

So much for caring about all of her boys. "We found signs of a fight," I said.

"Oh, I'm sure it's got nothing to do with Dewey." Puddles licked her thumb and wiped a smudge off Dewey's cheek. "He doesn't like to fight."

"He liked to fight last night," I said.

Puddles finally released her hold on Dewey and turned to me, a scowl on her face. "What are you suggesting?"

"I'm suggesting your precious nephew might have hurt Serath."

"It was a disagreement," Dewey whined. "No one got hurt."

"You heard him. They had a small disagreement. A bit of rough and tumble, like boys always do. It's nothing to concern yourself with. And you shouldn't have involved the angels."

I gaped at her. "Less than an hour ago, you were off to force the angels into action because you couldn't find Dewey."

She flapped a hand at me. "I overreacted. It's not important now. Not now I have my baby back." She rained kisses on Dewey's cheek while Bart looked on with sly amusement.

Dazielle walked over and nodded at Puddles. "There are signs of a struggle. We think the blood on the ground is not from an animal."

"Whatever happened here, it has nothing to do with Dewey, does it?" Puddles looked at her nephew, whose face was smeared in her sticky pink lip gloss.

"Of course not, Auntie. Serath is a friend of mine."

"There you go," Puddles said as if that settled the matter.

"We need to talk to you both." Dazielle addressed her comment to Dewey and Bart.

"They will co-operate if they must, but they have nothing to do with whatever you're looking at here," Puddles said. "Come on, boys. It's time we left. You look like you need a bath with plenty of bubbles and a big breakfast after your adventures."

"An adventure where one of their friends went missing." I glowered at Puddles, but there was nothing I could do to stop her from taking them away. No one was claiming they'd been injured, and there was no sign of Serath, so the blood might not even be his.

I looked around and noticed Rhett had slipped away as soon as the angels arrived. He was not a fan of Angel Force. I guess I'd never find out what he was doing skulking around in the forest. It was probably better that way.

I sighed as I watched Puddles go. At least she had her nephew back and would stop hassling me to find him.

Before I had a chance to walk away and seek out my own delicious breakfast, a hand landed on my shoulder.

"Tempest, we need a word," Dazielle said.

I gritted my teeth as I turned to Dazielle. "This isn't my business. I was helping Puddles find her nephew. Now she's done that, I'll leave the rest to you. As you said, you're the expert."

Dazielle shook her head. "Let's have a chat over coffee."

"Did somebody say coffee and cake?" Wiggles raced over and bounced on his paws.

"Nobody mentioned cake," Dazielle said. "It's not even nine in the morning."

Wiggles glared at her, and his eyes flared red. "You call yourself an angel and you deny a hungry hound a treat. I was the one who found the murder scene."

"It's not a murder scene," I said.

Wiggles snorted. "Well, the scene of evil doings. You don't find blood like that and figure a fairy picnic went down."

"You might. Fairies can be spiteful," I said.

Wiggles nodded. "True. They have sharp teeth and attitudes, especially the ones with sparkles."

Dazielle sighed. "I'll see what I can do about cake, so long as you stop talking about fairies."

I was tempted but could not be swayed by the offer of cake for breakfast. "We've already eaten, and I've got a bed waiting. You can deal with this without me."

"I've no doubt I can." Dazielle arched an eyebrow. "However, you were one of the last people to see Serath before he vanished."

I took a step back. "You're thinking I've done something to Serath?"

Dazielle nodded sagely. "Let's go to the cafe. All I want to do is find out what you know."

It looked like it would be cake for breakfast after all. I grudgingly followed her through the trees with Wiggles as we left the other angels at the scene and headed to the Unicorn's Trough.

Dazielle was true to her word as we settled at a table. She ordered hot drinks and three large slabs of coffee and walnut cake.

I decided she should go first since she'd insisted on this interview. We had great fun staring at each other in tense silence as we waited for the food.

Brogan Costin brought over our cake and coffee. "Starting early on the sweet stuff, ladies."

"I need it. The angels are being spiteful." I cut off a large piece of cake and stuffed it in my mouth. I groaned at the perfect combination of sweetness and slightly bitter walnut.

Brogan grinned. "Let me know if you need anything else." He walked away from the table.

Dazielle ate her own cake, sipping on her coffee delicately as if showing me how a person with table manners ate.

I felt a little better after I'd finished my cake. I sat back and raised my eyebrows. "Okay, question me. What do you need to know?"

"Are you friends with Dewey Lavern and his buddies?"

"Definitely not. I grew up with Dewey. He always played the fool and never took anything seriously. I haven't seen him for over a year. He comes to visit Puddles, but I think it's because he gets his arm twisted by his mom. I don't think he enjoys his visits."

Dazielle nodded. "I'm also not a fan of Dewey Lavern. He's got a record, you know."

I leaned forward. "I didn't know that. What's he done?"

"It mostly involves his inability to hold his alcohol. A few fights, nothing serious."

"Dewey needs to grow up."

"I don't disagree." Dazielle placed her mug down. "Puddles informed us you threw them out of Cloven Hoof last night."

I grimaced. Puddles needed to learn to keep her mouth shut. "They were hassling the customers and staff. When Dewey started on me and Axel, I decided that was enough. It was all above board. They were given fair warning. They threw the first punch, and Suki and I ended the fight."

"I heard Dewey say something about an argument over a girl."

"I know nothing about that. They annoyed nearly everyone they spoke to in Cloven Hoof. I should never have allowed them in."

Dazielle brushed crumbs off her fingers. "We should head over there and speak to your staff."

I checked the time. "I'll speak to my staff. It will only be Merrie there this early."

"Your bar manager?"

"That's right."

"Then she should have seen what happened. She can shed light on who Dewey and his friends were sweet talking."

I grimaced. I didn't want Dazielle, or any of her angels, poking around Cloven Hoof. "She'll help if she can. But it will be easier if I ask the questions."

"Why? Does Merrie have something to hide?"

"Merrie is one of the most honest people I know. If there's anything useful to tell, she'll reveal it."

"We're going now," Dazielle said. "The sooner we find Serath, the better."

"He's drunk and asleep in the forest. Go look for him there."

"Most likely he is, but we need to make sure, especially if Puddles is involved. She can be a little... trying."

I couldn't argue with that. "Puddles doesn't seem worried now Dewey is safe."

"I like to be thorough."

"You're wasting your time thinking anyone at Cloven Hoof is involved in Serath going missing," I said as we left the Unicorn's Trough and walked along the main street toward my bar. "I vet my staff. I trust them all."

"I'm sure you do, but it doesn't hurt to ask." Dazielle glanced at me. "And I hear you have a new batch of Mexican dried mushrooms in stock."

"Do you want a taste test?"

"How kind of you to offer. That's put me in a good mood, so I won't be too tough on your staff."

I snorted a laugh. Who knew angels could be so devious?

As we entered Cloven Hoof, I spotted Merrie behind the bar. Her smile dimmed, and her gaze cut to Dazielle. "Is everything okay?"

"It's nothing to worry about," I said to her.

"It is something to ponder, though. A customer has gone missing," Dazielle said. "I need to know what your involvement is."

So much for her not being tough on the staff.

Merrie's eyebrows shot up, and she lowered the glass she was holding to the bar. "Who's disappeared?"

"Serath Duckle," I said. "Dewey Lavern's friend. He was the tall, blond one."

Dazielle slid me a glare. "What can you tell me about his activities last night?"

"Not much." Merrie glanced at me, and I nodded. We had no secrets to hide from Angel Force.

"What did he do? Who did he talk to?"

"He mainly spoke to his friends," Merrie said. "They'd had a lot to drink."

"Did they bother you?" Dazielle asked.

I headed around the bar and returned with some speciality Mexican mushrooms. I placed them in front of Dazielle and gave her a pointed look.

She shrugged and took a mushroom.

"It wasn't anything I couldn't handle," Merrie said. "Dewey was a bit suggestive, but I shut him down. They were sensible enough to know not to annoy the staff too much, or we'd have refused to serve them."

Suki strolled into the bar from the cellar, stretching her arms over her head. She froze when she saw Dazielle, and her eyes grew wide.

"Don't worry, Suki," I said. "She's not here for you."

"I do want to talk to you," Dazielle said. "You might have been the last person to see Serath before he disappeared."

Suki slowly lowered her arms. "Serath?"

"He was one of those three guys we tossed out of here last night," I said to her. "One of them has gone missing."

"And we've found evidence that suggests he may have been injured," Dazielle said. "In the forest. The forest you know extremely well."

"Hey, no interrogating Suki." I grabbed the mushrooms away from Dazielle. "She's not involved with this. And you know what happens when Suki gets nervous."

Dazielle shifted in her seat. She'd been knocked on her behind by Suki before. "What did you see after you threw them out of Cloven Hoof?"

Suki twisted a long dreadlock around one finger. "Nothing! They walked away. It looked like they were arguing, then the blond one walked off on his own. They didn't come back. I wouldn't have let them in if they had."

"Serath is most likely licking his wounds somewhere," I said. "He's sulking after the fight."

"Maybe those wounds are too severe for him to lick," Dazielle said.

"Or he could have left Willow Tree Falls," I said. "Serath didn't want to hang around with Dewey and Bart, so he left early."

"Did he speak to any other bar staff while he was here?" Dazielle asked.

"He had a few words with Izzie," Merrie said. "When I realized they were a handful, I took over and served them. The girls don't need to be hassled."

"What words did Serath say?"

"The stupid words drunken guys say when they're trying to impress their friends. It was nothing.

Besides, the team can handle boys like Dewey and his friends. We do it almost every night."

The snow globe on the bar shook, and I activated it.

"Tempest, you need to come take a look at something."

I was surprised to hear Rhett's voice. "What's up?"

"I think I've found Serath, and he's not looking good."

"You found our missing guy?" Dazielle butted in on the conversation.

"Oh, you're with Angel Force." Rhett sounded cautious.

"Don't worry about that," I said. "Where's Serath?"

"In the woods. By an old gnarled oak tree that looks like it has an owl carved in the trunk. Close to the swamp."

"I know where you mean," I said. "We'll be there soon. Don't let Serath go anywhere."

"I don't need to worry about that. Tempest, he's dead."

Chapter 5

Dazielle flew ahead of me as I ran along the streets with Wiggles by my side, back to the forest.

"I knew something bad had happened to that guy," Wiggles said. "All that blood and mess on the ground, you don't get that playing hide 'n' seek."

"Serath was a jerk, but he didn't deserve to die," I said.

"He must have carried on his argument with his buddies, and it went too far."

"Maybe." I entered the forest and sped along the path. I soon spotted the white flare of Dazielle's wings as I pushed past a bush.

She stood at the edge of a shallow pit next to Rhett, who shifted from foot to foot and kept glancing at Dazielle as if expecting her to arrest him at any second.

I joined them and gulped as I looked down. In a grave lay Serath. His eyes were open as was his mouth, a look of terror forever pinned to his face.

"He did not go quietly," I muttered.

"That guy died screaming." Wiggles sniffed around the edge of the shallow grave. "And whatever magic was used on him stinks."

I nodded. It was unmistakable. Someone had killed Serath using dark magic. A bitter, sour smell drifted off his body.

Dazielle turned her attention to Rhett. "How did you know he was here?"

Rhett shrugged as he backed away, his hand shoved in his jeans pockets. "I know the place well."

"Well enough to know when someone has buried a body?" Dazielle stalked after him, her wings fluttering.

He glanced over his shoulder. "Sure. It's easy when you know how to follow the clues."

I hid a smile behind my hand. Angel Force was not known for following the right logic nor the correct clues when solving mysteries. It was how I often found myself dragged into their more difficult cases.

"What's your relationship with the victim?" Dazielle asked Rhett.

"No relationship. I have nothing to do with this guy." Rhett looked at me, the plea for help clear in his eyes. "I need to get out of here."

"Are you late for the office?" I asked with a grin.

A small smile crossed his face. "Something like that."

"Where were you last night?" Dazielle persisted.

Rhett raised a hand. "With the guys. They'll all vouch for me."

Dazielle scowled at him. "I will be in touch with more questions if I think you're involved in this death."

"I'm not. I'm trying to help. I didn't need to tell you I found Serath. Don't drag me into this investigation." Rhett scowled at Dazielle.

"I won't drag you anywhere if you have nothing to do with Serath's death." Dazielle's wings fully extended, a signal she wanted Rhett to know who was in charge.

He glanced at her wings and shook his head. "Whatever you say. You know where I am." Rhett turned on his heel and strode away.

Dazielle stared after him before returning her attention to Serath. "What do you think about Rhett?"

I watched him leave, trying hard not to leer at how well his jeans fit him. "You know what he's like. His gang runs on the dark side, but he keeps them in line. I don't think they had anything to do with this murder."

Dazielle snorted. "You need to take off those rose-tinted glasses. Rhett is not such a sweetheart."

I shrugged. I knew that.

"And curses?" Dazielle asked. "Something dark was used on Serath. Would the gang stoop to using a curse on someone who upset them?"

"It's possible, but anyone good at magic can conjure a curse. If you're looking for suspects based on that, you'll have to interrogate half of Willow Tree Falls."

"Let's hope it doesn't come to that."

Two angels descended from the sky, curling their wings behind them as they landed elegantly and strode over.

"Secure this scene," Dazielle said. "And have Serath taken away. We might find something on him that points to his killer."

The angels nodded and got to work.

Dazielle turned to me. "You can help with this."

I narrowed my eyes. "How do you want me to help?"

"You know Puddles."

I grimaced. "Because she's my landlady. I wouldn't call her a friend."

"Even so, you know more about her than I do. She will open up to you."

"About what?" I scratched my head. "You don't think Puddles is involved, do you?"

"You heard her when she found Dewey in the forest helping with our inquiries. She's protective of him."

"Sure, but we're talking about Puddles Lavern. Her worst habit is dying her hair every shade under the rainbow."

"Even so, we need to talk to her. Dewey, Bart, and Serath are staying at her house. Maybe she knows something about Serath or could have overheard them arguing when they were in their rooms."

"I won't be any help," I said. "You've got this in hand. Serath's been discovered, and your angels can figure out the rest."

"You're sitting in on the interview with Puddles," Dazielle said. "We need to get her talking."

I sighed but nodded. "Fine, the sooner we get this cleared up, the better. I don't want Cloven Hoof associated with dead bodies and curses."

"Exactly, and Puddles might tell us everything we need, and we can wrap this up by the end of the day."

I highly doubted it. I waited half an hour, throwing a stick for Wiggles while Dazielle did her official Angel Force thing, which mainly involved barking orders and stomping around fluttering her wings. Surely, those feathers must contaminate a crime scene.

Once she was done, we headed to Angel Force's headquarters, and Dazielle summoned Puddles to the station.

I was waiting in the reception area when she bustled through the door, dressed in a pale lemon suit.

"I came as quickly as I could," she said to me. "Dazielle said you have news about Serath."

I opened my mouth to tell her what was going on when Dazielle stuck her head into the reception area. "Best we do this in private."

Puddles turned her large eyes to me. "What's going on?"

"It's not great news," I said. "We'd better do what Dazielle says." I did not want to break the bad news alone to Puddles in case she got emotional.

Once we were settled in the interview room, Dazielle told Puddles about the discovery of Serath's body.

Puddles' hand flew to her mouth. "That's terrible news. That poor boy."

"Although we've yet to do a thorough investigation, we're certain dark magic was used on him," Dazielle said.

Puddles shook her head. "Who would want to harm such a charming boy?"

"That's what we need to find out. I'm curious. What would you do to protect Dewey?" Dazielle rested her hands on the table and fixed her gaze on Puddles.

"Dewey! Well, I'd do anything. He's my nephew. I love him."

"Do you love him enough to remove someone from his life that you consider a bad influence?"

"Oh! I see where you're going with this." Puddles' hands fluttered in the air as if she didn't know what to do with them. "You think I had something to do with what happened to Serath?"

"It's possible," Dazielle said. "You clearly feel the need to protect your nephew."

"Of course, but that's only natural. I didn't harm Serath." Puddles looked down at her lap. "Although, I did think he was a bad apple."

I leaned forward in my seat. "Why's that?"

Puddles sighed. "I didn't mean to pry, but I was tidying the boys' rooms after they went out last night and discovered something."

"You mean you were snooping around their stuff?"

Her eyes narrowed. "I like to keep a tidy house, and those boys are dreadful at keeping things neat. Anyway, I was looking around and discovered, well, let's say some items that make me think Serath was not such a nice boy."

"Was it pornographic?" I asked.

"No! I will not have filth in my home."

"What was it?"

Puddles' expression grew serious. "Serath was using dark magic."

My mouth opened in surprise. I had not expected that.

"What did you find?" Dazielle asked.

"A book of spells, a pot of what might be graveyard dust, and some human hair."

I sat up straight. "This guy isn't playing around."

"I would never have allowed him in my home if I'd known he was into such horrors. He must have fallen in with a bad crowd. Perhaps my Dewey felt sorry for him and was trying to get him on the right path."

"Or maybe your Dewey is also using dark magic?" I said. "He could have used some on Serath last night."

"Absolutely not! Dewey is high-spirited, but there's nothing wrong with that. He would never do anything to harm a friend. He's a good boy."

From what I'd seen of Dewey and his friends, they were definitely not good.

"Do you know of anybody who has a grudge against Serath?" Dazielle asked. "Anybody who would not be happy to see him in Willow Tree Falls?"

Puddles tapped her fingers on the top of the table. "You need to speak to that barmaid of yours," she said to me.

My head jerked back. "Which one?"

"Izzie. Serath has been involved with her." Her top lip curled as if she smelled something bad. "Maybe Serath upset her, and when she saw him back in Willow Tree Falls, she decided to do something about it."

I shook my head. I had no clue about this alleged relationship. "No way. Izzie isn't a killer."

"How well do you know Izzie?" Dazielle asked me.

"I know her well. Do not drag Izzie into this. Puddles is deflecting to get the heat off Dewey."

Puddles smoothed her hands over her hair. "As if I'd do such a thing."

I glared at Dazielle. "Izzie is reliable and a hard worker. I do not want you chasing away a good member of my team." I knew what Angel Force was like when they got the sniff of a suspect. They wouldn't let it drop, no matter how ridiculous it was.

"She wasn't there today when we spoke with Merrie," Dazielle said. "I need to talk to Izzie, especially if she knows the victim."

"If they did date, which I don't believe, I doubt Izzie even remembers Serath," I said. "His buddies said he's lousy with women. In fact, if they did date, I bet she only dated him because she felt sorry for him. Izzie is kind like that."

Dazielle shook her head. "I will talk to her. Unless you'd rather I bring her in and make it more official."

I groaned. "No, don't do that. Drop by the bar tonight. She'll be working." And I would definitely be there. I was not having Dazielle and her feathered crew annoying my staff.

"Izzie could have argued with Serath and things got out of hand," Puddles said smugly.

"Stop talking. You're making this worse," I said.

"Not for Dewey." Puddles' smile was on the wrong side of sly.

"Izzie would never curse a person," I said.

Puddles shook her head. "Whoever did this, it's a bad business. Even though Serath may have lost his way with his magic, I was fond of him. Deep down, he was a good boy. I hope you find whoever killed him quickly."

"Since you were so fond of him, you won't mind me asking where you were last night?" I asked.

Puddles puffed out a breath. "Of course not. I stuck to my usual routine. I had my dinner, listened to a little music while I did some lacemaking, and then went to bed. I had to be up early this morning to show a new rental to a couple."

"Did you share your bed with anybody?"

Puddles' cheeks flushed. "You know I'm not married."

"That doesn't mean you can't share your bed with someone." I grinned at her.

She pulled herself upright. "No, I shared my bed with nobody."

"Which means nobody can confirm what you did last night." I jabbed a finger at Puddles. "She's as much of a suspect as Izzie. More so, because she has no alibi."

"Tempest, that's enough. For now, we accept Puddles' alibi," Dazielle said.

"Quite right," Puddles said. "Because that's what I did."

"What music did you listen to?" I asked, not willing to let her off so easily.

She blinked at me. "Gilbert and Sullivan."

I let out a disgusted sigh. Of course, that would be her favorite type of music. You'd never catch Puddles Lavern rocking out to some amazing guitar riff.

"I believe you, Puddles," Dazielle said. "You've always been a model citizen. I've no reason to think you're lying."

I snorted and crossed my arms over my chest. I had reasons to think she might not be completely honest, but with Dazielle in the room, there was no point in pursuing more questions. Puddles' pastel-tinted reputation had saved her.

"That's all we need for now," Dazielle said. "Sorry to take up your time."

"That's quite all right. I'm happy to help any way I can."

I remained in my seat as Dazielle showed Puddles out. As much as I hated to admit it, I couldn't imagine Puddles killing a fly, let alone a person. But I wasn't going to forget about her, especially if Dazielle was interested in grilling Izzie and trying to get her to take the blame.

Dazielle walked back into the interview room. "So much for your help."

I shrugged. "Puddles was being smug. I prodded her to see if she had a temper."

"We need to return to Cloven Hoof and see what Izzie knows."

"Don't pin your hopes on Izzie being your killer. I agree Puddles is the most unlikely murder suspect in the village, but she has a connection to Serath."

"As does Izzie, by the sounds of it," Dazielle said. "Will she be at the bar by now?"

I checked the time. "Not until later. Drop by after eight, and we'll all be there. You can question her before the place gets too busy."

"Okay, but don't go talking to her until then."

"What do you think I'm going to say?"

"You might warn her that I'm coming so she gets her story straight."

I glowered at Dazielle as I shoved back my chair and stood. "Her story is already straight. She has nothing to do with this."

As I left Angel Force and walked away with Wiggles, I knew I'd have to stay involved in this case. I always hated it when Dazielle got that gleam in her eye when she thought she'd found the perfect suspect. She had that look now, every time she talked about Izzie.

She thought Izzie was guilty, but I knew she was wrong. I would not let an innocent person go down for this. I was hanging onto this case until we found out who the murderer really was.

Chapter 6

"Tempest! It seems like an age since I've seen you."
Mom engulfed me in an enormous hug before I'd
even stepped foot through the doorway of the house.

"I saw you two days ago." I returned her hug.

"That's too long. Come through. Dinner's almost
ready. Hello, handsome." She tickled Wiggles under
the chin, and his tongue rolled out with pleasure.

Everyone was already at the table when I arrived.
The only person missing was Auntie Queenie, who
must have the shift at the cemetery.

"We want to hear all about the murder." Granny
Dottie patted the empty seat next to her. "I hear
you've been spending a lot of time with the angels."

I shook my head as I settled in the seat. "Out of
necessity, not choice. Dazielle's got it in her head that
someone at Cloven Hoof is involved."

"Oh dear, that's not good news." Mom placed a
plate of spaghetti bolognese in front of me before

passing around everyone else's food.

"It's no one there," I said. "I trust my staff."

"The gossip is that you had Puddles in for questioning," Granny Dottie said. "What's that naughty thing done this time?"

"Your gossip is good." I swirled spaghetti around my fork. "She's crazy protective over Dewey, and I wondered how far she'd go to keep him safe. The problem is, she's squeaky clean. I couldn't muster up the belief she'd kill anyone."

Granny Dottie chuckled. "Puddles wasn't always such a good girl."

I raised my eyebrows. "She wasn't?"

"Absolutely not. She dabbled in the dark stuff when she was a teenager. It got her in a lot of trouble." Granny Dottie slurped a long string of spaghetti and smacked her lips together.

"Wow! You'd have no idea to look at her," I said.

"She doesn't touch the stuff now," Granny Dottie said. "At least, I didn't think she did. But maybe she cursed this boy. She'd know how to evoke a curse like that."

"Don't go spreading those rumors." Mom settled at the table. "You don't want Puddles coming after you with her voodoo dolls and pins."

Granny Dottie grinned. "I could take care of her if she caused me trouble. Anyway, her mom sent her away for rehabilitation. Puddles came back a reformed witch. She's no longer interested in dark magic. In fact, she became sickeningly good. She lost her spark."

I bit into a piece of warm homemade garlic bread as I considered this news about Puddles. Perhaps she still had a dark side and hid it under her pastel colors and bright hair. But she was such a goody two shoes, nobody could keep up such a good act.

"You must make sure this murder is tidied up quickly," Mom said. "Your cousins are coming to Willow Tree Falls in a couple of months. We don't want them to be too scared to visit."

I grinned. My cousins, Raine and Azura, were great fun, and I hadn't seen them for almost a year. "Don't worry. It'll be figured out soon enough. Serath's friends have to be involved. Dewey and Bart both looked like they'd gone a few rounds when I found them, and they seemed confused about what happened with Serath. I just need to convince Dazielle not to hound my staff and focus on legitimate suspects, and it will get sorted."

"And you don't want Cloven Hoof to be the center of a murder investigation," Aurora said.

I nodded. "No kidding. My business's reputation is at stake, and I'm not having the angels ruin it by lurking around and asking inappropriate questions."

"You'll get it figured out," Granny Dottie said. "We know how to whip those angels into shape when they make a nuisance of themselves."

I scooped up the last of my spaghetti. "Speaking of which, I need to head to Cloven Hoof. Dazielle will be there soon."

"I'll come with you." Aurora jumped from her seat.

I grinned at her. "Are you sure?"

"Absolutely, it's been a while since I've been at the bar. So long as that's okay with you."

I nodded. It was fine with me, but I knew that Aurora was really checking in on Frank to see how he felt about us hanging out. Frank had been quiet, and other than a few annoying belches, he hadn't bothered me for days.

We said our goodbyes and hurried out of the house with Wiggles.

Aurora practically skipped along the road as we walked and kept giving me sideways glances.

"What gives? Cloven Hoof is an awesome place to hang out, but it doesn't usually make you this happy when you visit."

Aurora grinned at me. "Toby is going to be there."

"Your secret squeeze?"

"He's not so secret. It's just that I still haven't told the rest of the family."

"I didn't think Cloven Hoof would be his sort of place." Toby Matlock was more of a private members club person.

"He's happy to go there if I am," Aurora said. "I think it will be nice if we spend time together, and you can get to know him."

I was cautiously intrigued about Toby. I didn't know much about him other than that he was a lot older than my sister, a powerful warlock with the ability to manipulate a person's thoughts, and under investigation by Angel Force for illegal magic activity. I did want to get to know him better. It seemed he was a permanent fixture in Aurora's life, and I needed to give him the once over and make sure he was good enough.

"Sounds great. I'll deal with the angels, and we can spend a bit of time together."

Aurora grabbed my arm and squeezed. "He's lovely. Toby is so romantic and such a sweetie. I think I'm falling for him."

"Are you sure you're ready to get serious? I mean, you're not that old. There's plenty of time to date other people before you settle down."

Aurora laughed. "Age doesn't matter. Toby's serious about me, and he's good for me. That's the main thing. Just you wait. When you get to know him, you'll love him as much as I do."

"Hopefully not as much as you do, or that will be weird."

She laughed again. "You know what I mean. Once you see how great Toby is, you'll understand why I'm so happy. It might inspire you to make a decision about your own love life."

"What love life?"

"Exactly my point. You've got two gorgeous suitors waiting in the wings."

I shrugged. "I have no idea who you're talking about."

Aurora tilted her head. "Of course you do. You're resisting getting attached. It's not so bad letting your guard down. I've never been so happy since I opened my heart to Toby."

"We can discuss my love life another time." I pulled open the door to Cloven Hoof and grimaced.

Dazielle and two other angels were already in the bar. They had an annoying habit of always being early for things.

I strode in and noticed several nervous looking patrons glancing at the angels. It was time to deal with them and get them out as quickly as possible.

I walked over to Dazielle. "Gather your feathery friends and let's grab a booth out of the way."

Dazielle smirked at me. "I've noticed a few people looking worried. Do you think they're doing anything illegal?"

I scowled at her. "I'm sure they're not. You being here is unsettling. Let's move our conversation to the back of the bar, and we can get this over with." I nodded to Aurora as she sat at the bar. "I won't be long."

"Take your time. I'll stay here and look out for Toby."

Once the angels were settled and no longer bothering my clients, I grabbed Izzie. "I hate to do this to you, but the angels want a word about what happened last night."

Izzie nodded. "I've heard the latest. Something about a curse?"

"That's right. And Puddles mentioned that you dated Serath."

Izzie's eyes widened. "For about five minutes a million years ago."

"Tempest," Dazielle called. "We're asking the questions over here."

I shook my head. "You've got nothing to worry about."

Izzie licked her lips. "Are you coming with me? Those angels make me nervous."

"Absolutely. I won't let them loose on you. I know what they're like."

She let out a sigh. "Okay, I've got nothing to hide. I'll talk to them."

I ordered a round of lemon drops from Ginger, and we walked over and settled in the booth opposite the angels.

"Tell me what you know about Serath," Dazielle said.

Izzie nodded. "Not that much. I wasn't all that impressed with him."

"You dated in the past?"

"Sure, but not for a long time. Serath said all the right words, but I soon figured he was a player."

"What did he do to make you realize that?"

"He cheated on me," Izzie said.

"That jerk," I said.

"Indeed," Dazielle said, that worrying gleam in her eyes again. "Go on."

"We met when he came for a visit with Dewey a few years ago. They were staying for a couple of weeks because his apartment was being decorated. Serath wasn't a bad-looking guy and caught my eye the first night he was here. We went out on four dates, and things seemed to go well."

"How did you discover he was cheating?"

"I was walking back from Cloven Hoof at the end of a late shift. I saw Serath stumbling out of the Ancient Imp, his arms wrapped around another woman."

"So, you were angry with him?" Dazielle asked.

"Of course I was angry. He was seeing other people behind my back."

"And you wanted revenge?"

I shook my head. It was so obvious where Dazielle was trying to force this.

"Back then, I would have, but that was years ago," Izzie said. "He came by Cloven Hoof the next night after I'd spotted him cheating, being all smooth and charming and saying how much he'd missed me. I dumped him on his cheating butt and never spoke to him again. Last night was the first time I'd seen him since then."

"And old feelings arose?" Dazielle asked.

"Hold on," I said. "Izzie has told you what she knows. You don't fall in love with somebody after four dates. She did the right thing. She ditched the loser and moved on."

Izzie nodded at me gratefully. "That's right. Sure, I wasn't thrilled to find him standing at the bar last night, but it didn't bother me. I could see he hadn't changed. I didn't want him dead, though. Nobody deserves that."

"You wouldn't have minded if you saw him with another woman while he was staying here?" Dazielle asked.

"I couldn't care less," Izzie said. "He's moved on with his life, as have I."

"Are you seeing somebody else?" Dazielle asked.

Izzie scowled at her. "Not at the moment. I'm happy to be single. There's no crime in that, is there?"

"Absolutely not," I said. "And Izzie was here last night. Dozens of customers will vouch for that, and so will I."

"We're still not sure exactly what time Serath was cursed," Dazielle said. "It's not outside the realm of possibility that Izzie cursed him in the bar and he died later."

"And then what? Izzie snuck into the woods, dug a shallow grave, discovered where Serath had collapsed after she'd cursed him, dragged him there, and shoved him in?"

Dazielle's eyes narrowed. "It's possible."

Izzie shifted in her seat. "Listen, I didn't like the guy, but I wouldn't kill him. He was being rude to a lot of people. Maybe he met his match after leaving Cloven Hoof. Someone could have jumped him, dragged him into the woods, and gotten their revenge. I don't know. All I know is that it wasn't me."

Ginger walked over with our lemon drops and set them down. "I didn't mean to overhear, but I was working behind the bar last night and heard everything Serath and his friends were saying. Izzie did nothing wrong, although she had every right to slap them."

"Do you know them?" Dazielle asked Ginger.

"No, I'm new to the village, but they were being disrespectful jerks. They were lucky Izzie didn't blast them off their feet for being so rude."

Izzie smiled at her. "I'm not going to deny I was tempted."

"They're not worth wasting your magic on," Ginger said. "They're not nice guys."

"Don't worry," I said to her. "Dewey and Bart won't get back in here again."

Ginger nodded as she walked away.

Izzie sighed. "She's right. I wouldn't waste my magic on a loser like Serath. I don't care about him. As far as I'm concerned, our relationship is ancient history. Besides, he'd gotten daft ambitions to get in with Rhett's gang. That can only mean trouble."

My eyes widened. "For real? Serath wanted to be a biker?"

"Absolutely. He was bragging about it last night. He even said they'd be lucky to have him."

Concern ran through me. Could that be why Rhett was in the woods when we'd been searching for Serath yesterday? Was he trying to cover something up? Had Serath showed off to the gang to prove he was worthy, and it went wrong?

"Have you got what you need?" I asked Dazielle. I needed to get out of here and speak to Rhett as soon as possible.

"For now," Dazielle said. "I might have further questions as this investigation continues."

Izzie shrugged. "I'll help if I can, but I don't know anything more than I've told you."

"Thanks, Izzie," I said. "You can get back to work."

She slid swiftly out of the booth and hurried away.

"Any chance you can get your angels out of my bar before you ruin the evening for all the customers?" I asked Dazielle.

Dazielle arched an eyebrow. "What's the hurry? We can stay for a few complementary drinks, make sure everyone is behaving themselves."

I glowered at her. "Aren't you on duty?"

She smirked. "I know what you're going to do. You're off to talk to your boyfriend and see what he knows about Serath's disappearance."

My plan had been rumbled. Dazielle was not as daft as she looked. "First off, Rhett's not my boyfriend. And second, why shouldn't I?"

"If you do, don't go feeding him any lines," Dazielle said. "And I'm only letting you talk to him because he shuts down every time he sees an angel. Anyone would think that guy has something to hide."

I shrugged. Rhett most likely did have things he didn't want the angels to know about. "I'm not going to help him cover up a murder, but a chat about his whereabouts and what he saw in the forest could be helpful."

"Sure. Let me know what he has to say." Dazielle gestured the angels to follow her.

I flicked her a salute. "Yes, ma'am."

Dazielle strode out of the bar with her angels in tow. The tension in the air vanished, and a buzz of conversation began as soon as the door had closed.

I raised my gaze to the ceiling. What was Rhett doing getting involved with Dewey and his friends? There was no way he'd want them in his gang. I couldn't let this wait. I had to speak to Rhett.

I hurried to the bar. "Merrie, I'm heading out for a couple of hours. Have you got everything you need?"

She smiled and waved me away. "You go. We're fine here. I've got Ginger and Blaze working tonight, as well as Izzie."

As I turned from the bar, Aurora stood in front of me, excitement on her face.

"I can't stop," I said.

Her smile faded. "Oh, just five minutes."

I looked at the door. I needed to tackle Rhett. "What's up?"

"I want you to meet Toby. He's just arrived."

I gritted my teeth, feeling torn. A part of me wanted to check out Toby and make sure he was legit, but I needed to get to Rhett and find out what he knew about Serath's murder.

"Please, it won't take long." Aurora tugged on my arm. "Toby is looking forward to meeting you."

I let out a sigh. "Sure, let's meet this guy and see just how amazing he is." My murder hunt would have to be put on hold while I checked out someone just as dubious.

Chapter 7

Aurora grabbed my hand and pulled me to a booth at the back of Cloven Hoof.

Waiting for us was Toby Matlock. He was a well-preserved warlock, who must be pushing fifty. He had slicked-back dark hair, a neat goatee beard, and wore a long purple velvet overcoat. He was trying hard to look like someone from a Victorian English murder mystery.

"Toby, this is my big sister, Tempest." Aurora gently pushed me toward Toby.

Toby extended a silver ring-covered hand. "It's a pleasure to be formally introduced."

I shook his hand. "I've seen you around Willow Tree Falls. I don't think we move in the same circles, though."

His smile was pleasant as he gestured for us to take a seat. "The Crypt family's reputation is an esteemed one. You are all well-known and liked in the village. I simply have not had the pleasure to spend time with your charming family, other than Aurora."

Oh, he was smooth. I perched on the edge of my seat as Aurora sat next to Toby. Toby was probably the wealthiest person in the village. He had expensive tastes, but then he could afford to.

"So, tell me how you met my sister." Since I was here, I may as well give Toby a decent grilling and see if I could make him sweat.

"I am a regular visitor at Heaven's Door. Aurora is usually far too busy to spend time chatting with me, so I had to bide my time before I captured her delightful attention."

She gently swatted his arm. "That's not true. I have time for all my customers."

Toby smiled at her and brushed a finger across her cheek. "One day, I was fortunate enough to be in the store when it was quiet. We got chatting, and she offered me an herbal tea. The next thing I knew, three hours had passed. Your sister is captivating."

I grinned at Aurora. "She has her moments."

Wiggles trotted over. He'd been sniffing around behind the bar since we'd arrived in the hope of getting food. "Are we done here? I'm in need of a long walk and a big, fat—"

"Is this creature yours?" Toby recoiled in his seat as he stared at Wiggles.

"I'm my own creature, buddy, and I can speak for myself," Wiggles said. "Who are you?"

"Wiggles, this is my boyfriend, Toby," Aurora said. "Tempest is getting to know him."

Wiggles tentatively sniffed the toe of Toby's black pointed boot. "Aren't you a bit old for Aurora?"

"He's the perfect age for me," Aurora said. "The guys I've dated in the past have been so immature."

"You deserve the very best, my dear." Toby's gaze was troubled as he watched Wiggles sniff around. "I did not know you had a hellhound as a companion," he said to me.

"It's a recent upgrade," I said. Toby was clearly not a fan of hellhounds. He squirmed and shifted in his seat like something cold had been dropped down the back of his shirt.

"It's an upgrade I approve of," Wiggles said. He fixed his fiery gaze on Toby. "Have you got a problem with hellhounds?"

"I'm not a fan of any animal," Toby said. "I have allergies."

"Oh, you poor darling," Aurora said. "I didn't know that."

Wiggles made a show of sitting and scratching until a cloud of fur drifted around him. There were times when I could kiss Wiggles.

"It's not a problem, so long as I don't spend much time with anything that has fur." Toby nodded at Wiggles.

"You've got no worries there." Wiggles trotted off, clearly not impressed by Toby.

Someone else who was also less than impressed with Toby was Frank. His hot energy curled up my spine, and I felt sweat break out on my forehead. The last thing I needed was Frank making an appearance and getting possessive over Aurora. Strangling Toby would not make a good first impression.

I shoved against his power until I was certain he was under control. "What are your intentions toward Aurora?"

"Tempest! You can't ask that," Aurora said.

"I can. How long have you been dating now, four months? That's enough time to get serious."

"I'm very serious about your lovely sister," Toby said. "She is flawless and beautiful, and she has the sweetest nature."

Aurora blushed and ducked her head. "I'm not that perfect."

I smiled. She was pretty near perfect, but her taste in men was questionable. Toby was very smooth, but the way he kept an arm around Aurora's shoulders hinted that he was possessive.

"I adore Aurora," Toby said. "If she allows me, I plan to be in her life for a very long time. You never know. You could end up being my sister-in-law."

Aurora gasped and stared at Toby. "Are you serious?"

"I believe we can be very happy together." He gently kissed her cheek.

I stifled a grimace. I'd never seen Aurora like this with a guy. She was quick to fall for hot looking guys, but her infatuations quickly cleared, and she moved on when the hotness fell away and there was nothing behind the muscles or cute dimples.

This relationship had been going on for a while, and all I could see was devotion on Aurora's face.

Could she really have fallen for this smooth-talking warlock? Maybe he was a father substitute. Our dad had been great, but he'd been missing for years. Aurora might have daddy issues we needed to discuss.

So far, I was undecided if I wanted Toby to become a part of the family. There was also the not insignificant issue of him being under scrutiny from Angel Force for illicit magic behavior. That would need sorting out before he came anywhere near the Crypt family.

Frank was still unhappy about Toby, and my stomach churned in the effort to control him. It was time to go. "It's good to meet you, Toby. Sorry, I have to cut this short, but I'm meeting somebody."

Aurora tore her gaze from Toby. "You're leaving so soon?"

"I have no choice. I'm helping the angels with this whole Serath problem," I said. "Rhett might be involved."

"That's not good," Aurora said. "You don't want to become a prison wife."

"A what now?"

"You know, visiting Rhett twice a month for a short conjugal visit. That can't be romantic."

"Hold on, Little Miss Marriage. First off, I'm not married to Rhett. We aren't even dating. Second, I'm not certain he did anything."

"Why are you suspicious about him?"

I sighed. "Rhett was in the forest when we were looking for Serath, and he found the body. I'm only talking to him so I can discount him."

"I am not fond of Rhett Blackthorn." Toby stroked his goatee. "Trouble follows wherever he goes. You would be wise to stay away from him."

"Thanks for the dating advice." I shuffled my behind out of the booth and stood. "I can handle Rhett and anyone else who comes into my life causing trouble."

Toby's smile was a picture of innocence. "I have no doubt about that. Aurora said you have a fire in your belly, as well as a demon."

There was something about this guy that set my teeth on edge. "Enjoy the rest of your evening." I hurried out of the bar with Wiggles before I said something rude to my potential future brother-in-law.

"What a sleaze," Wiggles said as he trotted along beside me. "Why is Aurora dating that idiot?"

"It's a good question," I said. "On the surface, he seems okay, but I don't know."

"He's okay if you like sleazy old dudes with terrible facial hair, who dress like they have a portal back to Victorian England they use to buy their clothes. What's with the frock coat?"

I laughed. "His fashion sense is questionable."

"And who sports a goatee? It's either a full beard or nothing if he wants to be on-trend."

I nodded. "There's a weird intensity between them."

"Toby stank of magic," Wiggles said. "I only had to sniff that ridiculous pointed boot to know it leaks out of his pores like last night's curry."

"He's got power. Some of it will seep out." I blew out a breath. "Frank hated him, as well."

"I agree with Frank on this one. Toby is not a cool guy for your sister to hang around with."

"Aurora seems genuinely in love. No guy has ever hung in there for more than a couple of months with her. She sees the next cute smile and moves on. Not this time. Maybe this is the real thing."

"Then the real thing sucks." Wiggles belched out a waft of brimstone fumes. "You need to have a word with Aurora and get her to see sense."

"Maybe I do." The trouble was, when Aurora talked about Toby, she got a glazed look in her eyes and started smiling like a moron. "I don't want to cause problems between us by telling her she's made a terrible dating decision."

"I'll do it," Wiggles said. "Anyone who doesn't like animals because they have allergies has no place in my life."

"You keep your dating advice to yourself. With a bit of luck, this relationship will burn out and Aurora will find somebody else."

"Someone younger with better dress sense and less goatee."

"Exactly." We entered the forest, and I hurried along an increasingly narrow path in my search for Rhett.

Rhett and his gang used the forest as natural cover, so they could do whatever dubious things biker gangs liked to do.

"There's someone up ahead," Wiggles said.

"Is it Rhett?"

Wiggles raised his nose and sniffed the air. "It doesn't smell like him. I'm getting a whiff of bike grease. Maybe it's another gang member."

"Let's see if he leads us to Rhett." I let Wiggles lead as he followed the scent trail. I soon caught a glimpse of a tall, broad-shouldered guy moving fast.

"I recognize him," I whispered to Wiggles. "That's Josh, one of Rhett's gang members." Josh was a huge, tattooed guy who knew how to work a beard.

We followed him deep into the forest for another fifteen minutes, the light almost disappearing as the trees overhead grew so thick.

Josh slowed, looked around, and ducked behind a large tree.

"What's he playing at?" I slowed and waited with Wiggles to see what Josh would do next.

After a minute, he emerged from behind the tree and walked away.

We hurried to the tree. It was an enormous ancient oak tree, its gnarled branches reaching up high into the sky. I ran my hand over the crumbling bark. "There's no magic attached to this tree. Have you got anything?" I asked Wiggles.

"Nothing down here, but there's a strange smell farther up above your head."

I lifted my hands over my head and felt around the tree. A piece of trunk gave way under my hand and pushed inward. I shoved my hand inside and found a wrapped package. I eased it out, placed it on the ground, and opened it.

"You have got to be kidding me." Inside the package was a selection of the dried mushrooms I specialized in at Cloven Hoof. No one else in the village had a license to sell these, so this stash was illegal.

Wiggles stepped back. "Phew, they are strong. I'm getting high from the fumes."

"I've warned Rhett's gang about selling this produce. He promised me it had stopped."

"You need to have another word with the gang," Wiggles said. "They didn't hear you the first time."

I blasted the mushrooms with a fireball, sending them up in a puff of smoke. Anger pulsed through me. Rhett had assured me his gang wasn't selling anymore, and I'd been dumb enough to believe him. I kicked the charred mushrooms across the forest floor.

I wasn't just angry. I was hurt. I trusted Rhett, and he'd lied to me. "Let's confront Josh about this. Maybe he's got more mushrooms stashed away that need a little fire magic applied to them."

Wiggles bounded ahead, and I was about to follow him when arms wrapped around me from behind and pulled me tight against a hard chest.

Chapter 8

"What the hell?" I kicked back against whoever was dumb enough to grab me from behind. My anger and panic excited Frank. His power burst up my spine and tickled the back of my neck, eager to get out and challenge this threat.

Whoever had hold of me grunted as my foot made contact with a shin, but they held on tight. "What are you doing here?"

I recognized that low, sexy voice, but Frank was desperate to get free. There was little I could do as his energy pulsed through me, sliding to the top of my head and bursting out.

The world took on its usual red tint as I saw everything through Frank's eyes. I was always stronger when Frank was in control and grabbed the arms wrapped around my chest and flipped my attacker over my head.

I knew it. It was Rhett. He landed on his back with a grunt, and his eyes widened as I pressed my foot into his groin. I say I did, but Frank was in control, and I could do nothing but sit back and watch, hoping he didn't annihilate Rhett.

"How dare you attack me," Frank purred.

"Tempest, get control of your demon," Rhett said.

"She does not need to control me. I have perfect control of myself. And I know exactly what I intend to do to you."

"Don't kill him," I said to Frank, the words sounding like an echo inside my head.

"Tempest wants me to save you," Frank said. "My little witch desires your pathetic form to remain alive. Is that what you'd like?"

"I'm not ready to die just yet," Rhett said. His eyes blazed with anger, but he was wise not to fight back against Frank.

"Yet you decided it was a sensible move to attack us?"

"You're in our part of the forest." Rhett grunted as my foot squashed harder into his groin.

"I didn't realize you owned some of our forest."

"Boss, we've heard back from Pete about the shipment." Two of Rhett's gang, Ian and Josh, appeared through the trees.

"Hey, what's going on?" Josh asked.

"Get out of here," Rhett yelled. "I've got a handle on this."

Frank chuckled. "Have you, now? This should be amusing."

"Tempest, what are you doing to Rhett?" Ian Blaine, a mean-spirited member of Rhett's gang, edged nearer, his eyes narrowed. Josh joined him.

"Oh please, make my day and jump me," Frank said.

Ian was not the brightest guy in the world, but even he must see I wasn't in control.

"I'm telling you to leave," Rhett said. "There's nothing going on here."

"There is." Frank hauled Rhett up by the collar of his jacket. "I want to play."

"No way. Josh, let's get her." Ian charged and threw himself at me.

Frank danced me backward, keeping me away from Ian's fists, but keeping hold of Rhett so he was dragged along the ground.

Josh dodged behind me and tried to grab me, but he was too slow.

Frank dropped me to the ground, so Rhett landed on top of me. He suckered my lips to Rhett and held on tight.

Rhett's eyes bulged, and he shoved against me.

I tried to scream a warning, but Frank was in command. He was trying to suck Rhett's energy out of him.

Josh grabbed Rhett by the back of his jacket and rolled him away. He held a large splintered tree branch, which he slammed toward my head.

Frank laughed as he flipped me away and launched me upright.

"Don't you dare!" I felt him snaking his power through my arm, conjuring fire.

"You should never dare a demon." Fire flew out of my hand and ignited the tree branch.

"Don't fight Tempest," Rhett gasped. "She's not in control."

Josh and Ian glared at me but made no more moves to attack.

Frank beckoned them closer. "Show me what you've got. I'm just warming up."

Ian crouched, but Rhett's barked order to stop kept him in place.

I fought to get back control. Frank should not be loose in Willow Tree Falls. Everyone I loved lived here, and he was dangerous.

Frank sighed inside my head. "I thought these biker guys were supposed to be tough. Where's the magic? Where's the anger? All I'm seeing is attitude."

"Rhett didn't mean to surprise me," I said as we carried on a conversation inside my head. "We don't need you."

"You make a demon feel unloved. I'm not done yet." Frank's hot power seeped into my arms. I was propelled toward Ian and struck him on the side of his head. A fireball appeared in my palm, and it smashed down by Josh's feet.

Josh retaliated with a flare of lightning.

The air crackled, and the smell of burning hair filled my nose.

Rhett threw himself on top of me and rolled me in the dirt. "You're on fire!"

"Enough!" I gasped and wiped my hands down my face as I came to a stop by the base of a tree.

Frank's energy finally faded. He was either bored with the fight or didn't want me too badly injured. I favored the former option. My body shook, and I could taste dirt.

"How are you doing, Tempest?" Rhett remained crouched by me, blood seeping from a wound on his head.

Frank pulsed at the back of my neck. "Give me a minute. Nobody make any sudden movements."

Wiggles trotted over. "That was fun."

"Fun! Where were you when I needed your help?"

"You had things under control. You did a great job. Or should I say Frank did an awesome butt-kicking job?"

"You could have warned me about Rhett being around," I said. "I could have kept Frank under control if I'd have known he was about to grab me."

"You have nothing to worry about when it comes to Rhett. He's in love with you. He'll never hurt you."

Rhett looked over, surprise in his eyes, but he didn't challenge Wiggles on that statement.

I groaned and hid my face in my hands for a second.

"Is everything okay now, Tempest?" Rhett's tone was cautious.

"My idiot demon will not attack anymore if that's what you're asking." I pulled myself to my feet. "But everything isn't okay. Your gang is selling off-limits supplies. I've warned you about this."

Surprise registered on Rhett's face. "They're not."

"I just destroyed a bundle of dried mushrooms I found stashed in the tree by one of your guys."

Rhett turned to look at his wounded gang members. "Is this true? Has anyone been selling produce?"

Ian shuffled his feet and looked around.

Josh cleared his throat and stepped forward. "Boss, there's been a misunderstanding. We have been selling produce, but it's not what you think."

"It looked exactly like the dried produce I sell at Cloven Hoof," I said.

"Sure, and that's what it's supposed to look like," Josh said. "Boss, I wouldn't break my word."

Rhett stood and brushed down his black jeans. "What have you been selling?"

"It's not legitimate stuff. You don't get the same buzz off it as you do Tempest's goodies."

"You're selling fake mushrooms?" Rhett asked.

Josh nodded. "That's right. And not to locals, just visitors. They get a short buzz but nothing else. I make it good and stinky, so they think they're getting something strong. They don't know the difference."

Rhett shrugged and glanced at me. "Technically, Josh isn't breaking any rules."

I glowered at Josh. "That's not the point. We had an agreement. You don't sell dried mushrooms, even if they aren't the real deal."

Josh tipped his head back, a guilty look on his face. "It was a good way to make extra cash. I didn't mean any harm. And if any of the locals came to me, I'd send them to your bar. I know not to tangle with you or your family."

I guess that was something. "Who have you sold to recently?"

Josh looked at the toes of his boots.

"Answer her," Rhett said.

Josh sighed. "That guy who was found dead and his friends. They came into the forest and were making such a racket as if they wanted to be found."

"All they wanted was dried mushrooms off you?" I asked.

"Not to begin with." Josh smirked. "What they wanted was to join the gang. Well, actually only Dewey was interested in that. He was bragging about what a big man he was and how we should welcome him. He kept on about his contacts and ideas he had for making money. He was a joke."

Ian chuckled and nodded.

"There's no way we'd have Dewey Lavern join us," Rhett said. "He's not gang material."

I arched an eyebrow. "What happened after you rejected his application to join your special gang?"

"Nothing, they bought mushrooms and left the forest. I guess they headed to Cloven Hoof," Josh said.

I squinted at Josh, not totally convinced. Maybe the deal had gone bad and Serath came back to get a refund. Josh would not have been happy. Would he have been mean enough to kill? I could imagine him kicking Serath's butt, but murder, I wasn't certain.

"I trust Josh," Rhett said. "He's honest."

"There's nothing honest about Josh," I said. "He's been selling mushrooms behind my back."

"Not anymore," Rhett said. "That was a mistake."

"Boss, it's a great sideline," Josh said.

"Mushrooms are Tempest's territory. Is everyone agreed on that?"

Ian and Josh nodded.

I was still not satisfied. "What about Dewey's friends, Serath and Bart? What did you think of them?"

Josh shrugged. "They're not memorable. Serath was a jerk with a big mouth, like Dewey."

"And Bart?"

"He was trying to be the nice guy, being super friendly and patting everyone on the back. Then he got weird."

"Weird how?"

"He asked about getting a specific spell. He wouldn't say what he wanted at first. It turns out, he was after a seduction spell."

Ian and Josh both laughed again.

"A seduction spell! That's seriously sleazy magic."

"He wasn't the most charismatic guy," Ian said. "Maybe it's the only way he can get a girl."

"And I suppose you all have super-hot love lives?" I tilted my head and ran my gaze over Ian and Josh. "I don't see you fighting off gorgeous women with a stick."

The guys looked at the ground and shuffled their feet.

"No? Don't tell me. You're both single."

Rhett smirked. "Don't be mean, Tempest. The guys work hard. We don't all have time for romance."

"And you do any better?" I said. "It's been a while since I've seen a girl on your arm."

His gaze darkened. "I'm waiting for the right girl to make up her mind."

My cheeks heated, and I looked away. I'd walked into that one and deserved it.

"Tempest, I promise you, no more mushrooms," Josh said. "And we didn't do anything to Serath or his weird friends."

"One final question. On the night of Serath's murder, where were you?" I asked Josh.

"He was with us," Ian said.

I shook my head. Of course, they would use each other as alibis. It was less than perfect, but Josh had a whole gang on his side, and there was nothing I could do about it.

"Have you heard enough?" Rhett asked. "Or do you want to take us in for questioning?"

"I've heard enough for now," I said.

Rhett caught hold of my elbow and walked me away from Ian and Josh. "Tempest, you need to be careful coming into the forest on your own."

"I'm never on my own. I have Wiggles and Frank, as you've seen tonight."

Rhett rubbed a bruise on his cheek. "Yes, I'm intimately acquainted with Frank."

I shrugged. "At least I know your gang won't mess with me unless they want a taste of Frank's fist again."

"They already know that. They were protecting me." Rhett touched the broken skin on my knuckles and held my hand gently. "And it wasn't Frank's fist. It was yours. Your demon forgets you can be broken."

"He doesn't forget. He just doesn't care." I eased my hand from his grip. "I know they're your gang and you're loyal to them, but did Josh and Ian tell the truth? Dark magic killed Serath. Somebody out there has a serious amount of power. It's only going to get worse if they don't keep their powers in check."

"My gang is not involved in this. Josh told me about Serath and his buddies coming into the forest and him giving them the brush off. He didn't need to do that. Nothing freaky went down between them."

"And Josh really was with you the night of the murder?"

"He was. We were having a few beers and hanging out. He was there the whole time. We packed up just after midnight and headed home."

I nodded. It seemed unlikely that Josh would use such dark magic on someone who'd asked a few dumb questions.

Rhett and his gang were still on my radar, though. They knew these woods and might have seen or heard something and weren't connecting it to the murder, or didn't want to, in case it got somebody in trouble.

"Tempest, I'm happy to lend a hand if you want to find the real killer. I can ask around and see if anybody knows anything."

I shook my head. "It's fine. I don't need your help."

Rhett smiled tightly. "You always say that."

"Because it's always true." I turned and walked away. I couldn't get Rhett involved in this investigation, especially since he might be implicated in what had happened to Serath.

I needed to figure out the next step alone. No gorgeous biker allowed.

Chapter 9

I yawned as I rolled out of bed the next morning. My dreams had been full of images of Serath in the ground, with that frozen scream on his lips. I wished I'd never seen him like that.

Wiggles clambered to his feet from his bed in the lounge he occasionally used as I wandered in to make coffee.

He scratched his belly with a back paw. "What's for breakfast?"

"Dog kibble for you, and…" I looked in the fridge. A sad, wrinkled orange and a stale piece of cheese stared back at me. I went to the cupboards. "Hey! I've got chocolate chips. We can have pancakes."

"Excellent. Tip the dog kibble in the trash and let's do chocolate chip pancakes."

"The dog kibble stays. You can have one pancake, no chocolate."

Wiggles grumbled as he made short work of the bowl of food I gave him.

I set to work on the pancake batter as the coffee brewed. "I'm still no closer to figuring out what went on with Serath."

"My genius input is always available," Wiggles said. "If you give me two pancakes, I might crack this case wide open for you."

I nodded as I tipped the first batch of batter into the heated pan. "The obvious suspects are Serath's friends, Dewey and Bart."

"Yup. They were seen fighting after they left Cloven Hoof," Wiggles said.

"But when I discovered them in the crypt the next day, they seemed clueless."

"That could be their default position," Wiggles said. "Those two don't strike me as Einstein clever, more Homer Simpson on a bad day."

"But they fought. Dewey and Bart had injuries on their hands."

"Serath wasn't killed in a fist fight. He was killed by a curse," Wiggles said.

"Which means we're looking for someone with powerful magic," I said. "Someone who can handle the dark stuff without it eating them alive or, at least, doing an amazing job of hiding their true nature."

"And again, neither of those guys struck me as geniuses when it comes to magic use."

I flipped over the pancake. "There's also Puddles to consider. An ultra-protective auntie who'd do anything to keep her precious Dewey safe."

"And Puddles has a dark side," Wiggles said. "Maybe some of that darkness has slipped back, and she used it on Serath. It was a punishment for him bringing black magic paraphernalia into her house."

I pursed my lips as I watched the batter bubble. "She decided Serath was not fit to be around her nephew and got rid of him."

"There's potential in this theory. Puddles snuck out of her house late at night, made sure Serath was separated from everyone else, and then killed him," Wiggles said. "Then she dug a grave to put him in without anyone seeing what she was up to."

"Someone with a love of unicorn colors is never discreet, but it's not impossible." I flicked the first pancake out of the pan and cut it in half. "Puddles lives alone, so no one would have noticed if she did slip out."

Wiggles grunted, his gaze on the pancake. "Leave me at least one chocolate chip."

I shook my head as I picked them out of his piece. "I don't see Puddles skulking about in the forest and digging a grave. She'd break her pink nails."

"Maybe her unicorn colors are a front. She could be some bad-ass black magic-using witch just biding her time. Waiting for the right kind of sleazebag to come into her life so she can use her dark powers on him."

"Serath would fit that category." I set his chocolate free pancake down and sat at the table to enjoy mine alongside a freshly brewed mug of coffee.

"So, we're not scrubbing Puddles off the suspect list," Wiggles said.

"Not just yet. But we also have to consider her darling nephew, Dewey."

"A dodgy character."

"The problem is, he went off with Bart."

"Who is also a suspect."

"He is, although Suki swears she saw them both part company with Serath after they got flung out of Cloven Hoof."

"It doesn't mean they didn't meet up later," Wiggles said. "Maybe Dewey and Bart decided to get revenge against Serath and arranged to meet him in the forest."

"As you said, they don't come across as competent magic users. They didn't even use magic when they were fighting me."

"We've also got the big, bad, bearded Josh and his naughty mushrooms," Wiggles said.

I narrowed my eyes. "I'm still not impressed with him for doing that."

"It's clever," Wiggles said. "He's making money and keeping on the right side of your rules."

"It still doesn't look good. He's taking customers away from me."

"Only in the short term. When people realize his mushrooms don't work, they'll come back to you."

"I bet he's undercutting my prices, as well."

"Moving on from your obsession with Josh's mushrooms and back to our murder, could Josh have killed Serath?"

I let out a sigh. "I've always seen Josh as a gentle giant. His size is intimidating, but he's not as malicious as some of the guys Rhett runs with. I'd be surprised if he used such dark magic."

"And he has an alibi."

"Which can't be relied upon," I said. "The gang members will say anything to cover for each other."

"Which leaves us with nobody's favorite suspect, Izzie," Wiggles said.

"Not a chance. There's no way she used dark magic on Serath."

"We don't know what was said between them," Wiggles said. "Serath could have insulted her, and she hunted him down after work."

I scowled at him. "I thought you liked Izzie."

"I love Izzie. She gives the best belly rubs."

"No, it's not her. She was at the bar until the end of her shift. Serath could have already been dead before she even left Cloven Hoof."

Wiggles raised one ear. "Shall I pencil her at the bottom of the suspect list?"

"Use an invisible pencil. We're not hounding Izzie about this. But we need to check in with Angel Force and see who they're favoring before they arrest an innocent bystander like Granny Dottie."

Wiggles snorted. "There's nothing innocent about her."

I smiled. He was right there.

After we'd finished our pancakes, we headed to Angel Force. As I pushed open the door, I felt the air buzzing with excitement.

I glanced over my shoulder to where Wiggles was sitting outside, waiting for me. The angels still had the sign up saying no hellhounds allowed.

I hurried to the desk. "What's going on?"

Cassiel grinned at me, looking so pleased with herself she was almost floating with joy. "We've made an arrest."

"Who did you arrest, and for what reason?"

"Serath's killer."

My eyes widened. "Who do you think killed him?"

Cassiel glanced over her shoulder. "I should wait for Dazielle to update you. This is her arrest."

A flicker of worry ignited in my gut. The angels were enthusiastic, but they often got things wrong. "She won't mind. Who is it?"

Cassiel clasped her hands together. "Josh, from Rhett's gang."

I took a step back. "Are you certain? I talked to him yesterday. He's got an alibi."

"It can't be a good alibi. Dazielle is sure he's involved. And it might not just be him. The gang rarely works alone. This could be the opportunity we've been waiting for to take down the whole gang."

Rhett's gang was shady, but he was always clear. They weren't killers. "What evidence has Dazielle got that Josh did it?"

Cassiel chewed on her bottom lip. "You'll have to ask her."

I scowled as I tapped my fingers on the desk. This didn't feel right, and it was happening too fast. "I'd like to see Dazielle."

Cassiel frowned. "She's very busy. You'll have to wait. She wants to oversee Josh's interview personally."

"No problem. I'll wait." I needed to make sure the angels didn't charge the wrong person and leave a killer on the loose.

✥✥✥✥✥ ✥✥✥✥✥

After a long wait and several stale doughnuts that I shared with Wiggles, I finally got to talk to Dazielle.

"I can give you two minutes." Dazielle gestured me through and strode along the corridor.

I hurried after her. "I'm after information about why you arrested Josh."

She gestured to a seat in the main office before sitting opposite me. "He has a terrible reputation, a lousy alibi, and admitted to seeing the victim before he died."

"I don't disagree with any of that, but that doesn't make him a killer. My reputation isn't great, I don't have a fab alibi, and I also saw Serath before he died."

"Don't tempt me." Dazielle arched an eyebrow. "Or do you have something you'd like to tell me?"

"What I'm saying is that you need more than that to charge Josh."

"It makes him the most likely suspect, so far," Dazielle said.

"What does Josh have to say about it?"

"He's pleading his innocence. He said he knows nothing about it."

"Which could be true."

"Or he could have killed Serath and his gang is covering for him. Why the skepticism?"

"Because there are other people involved. Puddles, for example, she also has a lousy alibi and a dark past."

Dazielle gave an unangel-like snort. "Puddles Lavern has nothing dark about her."

"Not true. I've heard from a reliable source that Puddles dabbled in the dark stuff."

"Who's your source?"

I hesitated before answering. "My Granny Dottie."

"Had she been drinking when she told you this?"

"No!"

"Puddles can't be involved. Maybe she ran wild when she was young, but she's a model citizen."

"A model citizen who broke into my apartment a couple of days ago."

"She did? Why would Puddles do that?"

"Well, she might have had a key, and she might have been worried about where Dewey was, but that's beside the point. She did something illegal. It shows she can't be trusted."

"Puddles is your landlady. It's okay for her to come in during an emergency. That does not constitute a break-in."

"I didn't consider it an emergency. Nobody wants to be woken to find Puddles standing by their bed."

"That doesn't matter now," Dazielle said. "Josh is in custody, and we're questioning him. It's only a matter of time before he lets slip what happened."

I wasn't convinced. "So, this is over? You don't need my help?"

Dazielle glanced at the door. "We can handle things."

Annoyance shivered through me, but I was glad Cloven Hoof and my staff were no longer of interest to the angels.

I stood from my seat. "Let me know what happens with Josh."

"You'll hear about it soon enough." Dazielle already had her head buried in paperwork, making sure I knew I'd been thoroughly rejected.

I left the building and collected Wiggles from outside before heading to Cloven Hoof.

"Case closed?" Wiggles said as he trotted beside me.

"If you believe the angels and their incredible deduction skills," I said.

"I fear those beautiful creatures couldn't deduct their way out of a paper bag with a map, compass, magic spell to light the way, and an experienced guide."

"It seems too convenient. They discover Josh is involved and their attention lasers on him. They're ignoring anybody else, people who have better motives than Josh."

I pushed through the door of Cloven Hoof to find Merrie and Izzie behind the bar getting things ready for the evening.

"I've had good news," I said. "Angel Force has arrested someone for Serath's murder."

Izzie made a show of wiping her forehead with the back of her hand. "Thank the goddess. They're not chasing after me anymore?"

"No, not that they should have been anyway. The case is closed, according to Dazielle."

"We need to celebrate." Merrie grabbed glasses and a bottle of champagne.

Blaze and Ginger walked out of the back room, carrying cases of booze.

"Get over here you two," Merrie said. "Izzie is an innocent woman."

"As if you ever had any doubt," Izzie said.

"Not for a second." Merrie filled the glasses and handed them around.

"Here's to freedom," Izzie said.

"And here's to no more angels poking around," I said.

We all raised our glasses in a shared toast.

Merrie was pouring another round when the door opened behind me. I turned and saw Rhett walk in, his expression dark.

"I'll be back in a minute," I said to the others. I walked over to where he waited by the door.

"It's a little early for you," I said to him.

Rhett stuffed his hands into his pockets. "I need your help."

"I'm almost afraid to ask. What do you need me for?"

"You've heard Josh has been arrested for Serath's murder?"

"I spent most of the afternoon trying to get information out of Dazielle, but yes, she told me she thinks he killed Serath."

"He wouldn't do that."

I shrugged. "Josh was passing off fake goods. He's not squeaky clean."

"That was nothing. Just because he did that doesn't mean he's expanded his skills to murder. Josh wouldn't use a curse like that. He hates curses."

I tilted my head. "Is there anyone who actually likes curses? They never end well."

Rhett shook his head. "No, I mean his mom was killed with a dark curse. He was a teenager, and it happened in front of him. He swore off that kind of magic. He knows how toxic it is."

I blew out a breath. "I'm sorry to hear that. It still doesn't mean he's in the clear. Serath could have come back and confronted Josh about his dodgy goods and things got out of hand."

"That didn't happen. We weren't lying when we said Josh was with us the night of Serath's death."

"Even so, I'm not sure I can help you."

"Tempest, you must. He's innocent. You've dealt with Angel Force before, so you know how they work. I have to clear Josh's name."

I shook my head. "No, this has nothing to do with me."

Rhett's gaze cut to Merrie and the rest of the bar staff. "Your crew is in the clear, and that's all that bothers you?"

I bristled at his words. "Pretty much. Dazielle was pointing the finger at Izzie, so I made sure that stopped. And I can't see this place get a bad reputation. If rumors get around that people wind up in a shallow grave after a night out at Cloven Hoof, it will be lousy for business."

Rhett glared at me for a second before sighing, the tension seeping out of his shoulders. "I get it. You don't want anything to do with the shady biker gang. But I promise you Josh is sound. He didn't do this. Now that the angels have him in custody, they won't let him go. You know what they're like."

Unfortunately, I did. Even when they had the wrong suspect, they kept hassling them. "Talk to Dazielle. See if you can get her to keep asking questions. She might find new evidence that clears Josh. She made it clear she doesn't want me involved anymore."

"There's no way you're getting me through the doors of Angel Force." His intense gaze settled on me. "I know you go there."

"Not for fun. Dazielle is convinced she's got the right person."

"She's wrong. They don't have solid evidence against Josh."

"They must have something. She seemed smug, and that's never a good sign."

"Dazielle has a prejudice and hang-ups because Josh is a part of my gang."

I rubbed my forehead. I could see how Rhett was struggling to keep his frustration in check. He was convinced Josh was innocent.

The dilemma was, if I helped to clear Josh's name, it would mean spending time with Rhett, and I wasn't sure I was up to the challenge. I kept my distance for a reason. Could I risk getting involved and stirring up old feelings? Feelings he might not reciprocate.

"I'll get on my knees and beg if I have to." Rhett grabbed my hand. "I need you for this. I need to get Josh free."

I groaned. "Fine, I'll help. But not today. I've got this place to run."

"Let's meet tomorrow. We can go over everything you know. I will also talk to the other guys, and we can check out the place Serath was found, see if there's any evidence the angels overlooked. Whatever it takes, I will clear Josh's name."

"Great, you do that." I looked down at our clasped hands. This was going to be tough. "How about we meet tomorrow morning at Unicorn's Trough for breakfast?"

"Sounds good. I'll meet you there at nine."

"I'll be there." I could handle this. I would have to be on my guard now that we were working together, and I would not let any treacherous thoughts make me do anything foolish.

"Tempest, this order doesn't look right," Merrie called as she held up a delivery slip. "Did you mean to order twenty cases of Russian Ararat?"

"I've got to deal with this. I'll see you tomorrow," I said to Rhett.

"Looking forward to it." He turned and left Cloven Hoof.

This could go badly, but if an innocent man was being falsely accused, it was only right I helped set him free. I just had to remember this was business and not pleasure. I would not fall for Rhett.

Chapter 10

I strolled through the door of Mom's house and into the kitchen, where everyone was seated around the table.

"There you are," Mom said with a smile. "Pancakes as usual?"

I shook my head as I took a seat. "Just coffee today. I'm having breakfast with someone."

"Who are you meeting?" Aurora asked.

I glanced at her. I should lie. The second I said Rhett's name, they would all question me. Was it a date? Did I love him? When were we getting back together? I could do without that.

Aurora grinned at me. "Is this a breakfast date?"

"It's nothing. I'm helping Rhett because the angels have arrested Josh for Serath's murder."

"Oh, we heard about that," Granny Dottie said. "And now you're helping that charming young man make sure his friend doesn't go down for a crime he didn't commit. It must be love."

I repressed a sigh. "I can assure you it's not. Rhett asked for my help and twisted my arm until I said yes."

"How hard did he have to twist?" Aurora asked.

"Very." I accepted the mug of coffee Mom placed in front of me and glared at Aurora as I lifted it to my lips.

"It's about time you two got together," Granny Dottie said.

"Nope, I've been there and done that, and it didn't work out."

"Because you played too hard to get," Aurora said. "A guy can only wait around for so long."

"I never asked him to wait around at all," I said. "Rhett's a free agent. He can date whomever he likes." So long as he told me nothing about it and I never saw him with another woman, it wouldn't be a problem.

"He'd like to date you," Aurora said. "Whenever Rhett comes to Heaven's Door, he always asks subtle questions about you. He still likes you."

I was not getting dragged into this. "My relationship with Rhett is professional."

"That's why you've got lipstick on," Aurora teased.

"It's lip balm. I have chapped lips." I pressed my lips together, wishing I'd never bothered with the gloss I'd painted on them.

"There's also Axel to consider," Granny Dottie said. "A wealthy half-demon shouldn't be ignored."

"I didn't think you liked Axel," I said to her.

"Did you miss the bit where I said he was wealthy?"

"Money is not everything, old girl," Grandpa Lucius said.

"I know everyone says, if you find happiness, then money doesn't matter, but it certainly helps. I'd be less miserable driving a Lamborghini than I would riding a bicycle in the middle of winter; that's for sure. Try again, Tempest. What's wrong with Axel?"

"He's a little on the smarmy side. He flirts with everyone. He has a perma-tan. He dresses like a Miami vice cop."

"He wears way too much cologne," Wiggles said.

"That too." Although, I quite liked his aftershave.

"He also desperately wants to get into Tempest's pants. It's sad," Wiggles said. "I smell the testosterone every time he gets near. And one time, he was wearing tight-fitting pants, and I swear, his—"

"Okay, Wiggles. No one wants to hear about that."

He cocked an ear. "What? It's true. Axel gets all sweaty when he's around you, like he's seen a tasty bone he wants to chew on."

"Axel does not do that, but he can be a little handsy."

"That can all be overlooked if Axel is generous enough," Granny Dottie said.

"That's enough of that." Mom passed around platefuls of pancakes. "Tempest can decide who she dates."

"Thanks, Mom."

"I just wish you'd hurry up and make a decision," Mom said. "You don't want to get the spinster label. Once you're known for that, no man will look your way unless they want to count the number of cats you own."

"What's so wrong with being a spinster?"

"Spinsters have a nasty habit of disappearing," Mom said. "You know your history of Willow Tree Falls."

"You're talking hundreds of years ago, when women who didn't marry got burned at the stake for being witches," I said. "That never happened here. This is one of the few safe places for magic users."

"Don't be so sure of that," Granny Dottie said. "There was a rumor of single women going missing in the fifties. They were never found, and they all owned cats."

"I've never heard that story," I said. "Your made-up stories can't scare me into dating."

"Set foot outside of our little haven, and everyone has their eye on the single women," Granny Dottie said. "And you also have Wiggles. He makes things worse."

"What's wrong with having Wiggles?" I glanced down at him, his nose now buried in his pancake breakfast. "Loads of people own dogs."

"Spinsters surround themselves with animals. It's a fact."

"No, it's not. Besides, maybe spinsters like animals better than people. I know I do."

"It won't do you any harm to go on this date with Rhett," Mom said. "Knock those spinster rumors on the head before it's too late."

I groaned. "This is not a date."

Puddles burst through the kitchen door, her blue hair unbrushed and her blouse misbuttoned. "I'm so glad you're all here."

"Puddles!" Mom jumped from her seat. "What's wrong?"

"I'm terribly worried about Dewey," Puddles gasped. "He didn't come home last night."

I shook my head. "I wouldn't be worried. He has a habit of doing that."

"No, he doesn't." Puddles glared at me. "And after everything that happened to poor Serath, I'm concerned."

"Angel Force is convinced they have Serath's killer. Dewey is safe," I said.

"I need to make sure," Puddles said. "He went out last night with Bart. They were having a drink to remember their lost friend."

"I'm sure that's the only reason they were having a drink," I muttered.

Puddles continued. "I told them not to be late. I cooked Dewey his favorite meal. Bart came back alone just after midnight. I waited up to make sure they got in safe, so I was there when he returned. He said Dewey met someone and went off with her."

I placed my mug down. "You're right. It is unusual that any woman could be interested in going anywhere with Dewey."

"Tempest," Mom cautioned.

"My Dewey is a respectable young man," Puddles said. "He wouldn't go with some strange girl he'd just met. Why would he want to do that?"

"I can think of one reason." I raised my eyebrows at Puddles. "Did Bart say who Dewey went off with?"

"No, he didn't know her. Bart's not from around here, so he doesn't know many people."

"Dewey got lucky," I said. "Good for him."

Puddles' hand fluttered across her chest. "I can't believe that. It's so unlike him."

"Puddles, take a seat," Mom said. "Have you had breakfast? I've got spare pancakes if you're hungry."

"Oh, I'm not sure I can eat. I'm so worried." Puddles sat down and grabbed a fork.

"Why don't you try?" Mom placed the pancakes in front of Puddles, and after a second of staring at them, she tucked in.

"I'm sure Tempest is right. Dewey found a lovely young lady, and they spent an enjoyable evening together, most likely talking or discussing their favorite book." Mom returned to her seat. "You shouldn't be concerned."

"I'm trying not to be," Puddles said around a mouthful of pancake. "My nerves are on edge after Serath's death. I need to make sure Dewey is okay."

"Tempest will help you with that," Mom said.

I frowned at her. "I will?"

"Of course. When you're out today, keep an eye out for Dewey. Ask around and see who's seen him. Maybe he's taking this young lady to breakfast, and you'll bump into him when you're on your date with Rhett."

"It's not a…" I shook my head. There was no point in trying to convince them otherwise. They all thought I was having a breakfast date with Rhett, and nothing would change their mind. "Fine, I'll look out for Dewey today."

"Thank you, Tempest. Let me know when you see him," Puddles said. "I won't be able to relax until I know he's safe."

"Sure, I'll let you know." I finished my coffee and stood. "I need to get out of here."

"I'll come with you." Aurora stuffed the last of her pancake in her mouth.

"You want to come to Unicorn's Trough with me?"

"No, I need to get the store open. I'm heading in your direction. We can walk together."

We said our goodbyes and left the house, Wiggles trailing along behind us.

"So, what do you think about Toby?" Aurora asked.

I smiled. That was the reason she wanted alone time. I snitched my nose. I needed to handle this carefully. Aurora was into this guy, and I still hadn't figured out why. "He was very polite."

"Toby has lovely manners." Aurora grabbed my arm and bounced on her toes. "He wants us to live together."

I sucked in a breath. "Isn't that a bit sudden?"

"No, we've been seeing each other for ages. We spend a lot of time together as it is. It feels like a natural next step."

Frank's energy curled around my spine. I sensed he also hated the idea of Aurora living with Toby. I had to agree with him. I didn't like the way Toby treated my sister like a china doll rather than a person. His weird intensity around her freaked me out.

"You should put on the brakes. You haven't told anyone else about your relationship. There's a reason for that."

Aurora's bottom lip jutted out. "You know what they're like. You only mentioned having breakfast with Rhett, and they've practically married you off."

"From the sounds of it, you and Toby are practically married. Living with another person is a huge step."

"Why wait when you know it's right?" Aurora said. "He's so sweet to me and treats me really well."

"He's also old enough to be your father."

"He's mature and sensible. Toby is not like those silly boys I used to date. They were always more interested in checking their own appearance or my cleavage than making sure I was having a nice time. I like being spoiled. There's nothing wrong with that."

"I should meet Toby again. I didn't get to know him that well when we met in Cloven Hoof." If I did meet him again, it would give me a chance to grill him about this living together rubbish. Aurora was too young to settle down, especially with some old, dodgy magic user.

"I thought you liked him," Aurora said quietly.

"I didn't say I dislike him," I said. "I just can't imagine you with him forever. What do you have planned for your future together?"

"Toby has talked about children and maybe travel."

"He wants to take you away from Willow Tree Falls?" I shook my head. "You love it here. You have your business, your family, and friends. Why leave?"

"He's not taking me away from anything." She patted my arm. "Tempest, I'm in love. I want to spend the rest of my life with Toby."

Frank's energy shifted up my spine, suggesting he wanted to have input into this unsavory matter. I shoved him back down. He needn't worry. I was as unhappy as he was about the prospect of Aurora moving in with Toby.

"How about this? You come clean to the family about Toby and see what they think."

Aurora groaned. "I can't face it. It will be like the Spanish Inquisition. They'll ask thousands of questions and insist he comes to dinner."

"Which is super annoying, but it will help you get a perspective on this."

"I already have a great perspective on it." Aurora glared at me. "Anyone would think you weren't happy for me."

I wasn't, not really. Aurora deserved better than Toby. "What about your apartment above Heaven's Door? You've spent ages getting that place just how you like it."

"I can rent it out. It will give me a bit of extra income. Toby has a lovely house and said he's happy to share it with me."

"It seems he wants you to give up a lot. What's he changing so you can be together?"

"I don't want him to change anything," Aurora said. "I like him fine as he is. And he's not forcing me to do anything. I'm happy to give up the apartment so we can be together. It's hardly a sacrifice. I'm going from a two-bed apartment above a store to a detached house with two acres of grounds and its own swimming pool. I call that a spectacular upgrade."

"A pool would be nice. Is it heated?"

She smacked my arm. "Of course! And you can use it anytime you like."

I nodded slowly. There was still something about Toby that made my skin crawl. If I didn't get the chance to meet him soon, I'd have to do some investigating into Toby Matlock. I did not want my sister giving up everything for some guy, only for him to turn out to be shady and manipulative.

"Be happy for me, Tempest. This is the first guy in a long time who's made me feel great about myself."

I shoved down my reservations. Aurora did seem blissfully happy with Toby. "I am, and if he makes you happy, then that's great."

"Give him another chance. You'll love Toby once you get to know him properly." She squeezed my arm.

"I'm sure I will." Especially once I'd thoroughly investigated him and made sure there was nothing dodgy going on when it came to my sister.

"I must go," Aurora said. "There will be customers waiting if I don't open up soon." She waved goodbye as she hurried away.

I watched Aurora go. That was something else to add to my to-do list. But first, I needed to get through my not-breakfast-date with Rhett and see if we could figure out if Josh really was Serath's killer.

Chapter 11

"Where is he?" I tapped my fingers on the table. I'd been waiting at Unicorn's Trough for half an hour, and Rhett had still not shown.

"We really need to eat," Wiggles said. "I'm feeling faint with hunger."

"You're not the only one." I peered out the window, looking for Rhett.

Brogan Costin came over and re-filled my coffee mug for the third time. "Are you ready to order?"

I glanced out the window once more. I didn't know what Rhett's problem was, but I was done waiting. "Yes, we'll have two breakfast specials."

"With extra toast," Wiggles said.

"And extra hash browns," I said. "And a side order of pancakes."

Brogan chuckled. "You two have quite an appetite this morning."

"Same as always." I was eating my feelings, but I didn't care. Rhett had stood me up after hassling me yesterday to get my help.

"I could go look for him." Wiggles rested his head on my knee. "Maybe he overslept."

"Don't bother. This is the last time I help Rhett."

"You need to find a real man," Wiggles said.

"One who can tell the time would be perfect right about now," I muttered. I'd been stressing about this breakfast date with Rhett, and he hadn't even bothered to show.

"What you need is someone who will keep you on your toes."

I looked down at Wiggles. "Have you got anyone in mind?"

He sniffed the air. "Brogan is a perfect catch."

I smirked. "You love Brogan because he makes amazing breakfasts. I'm not getting involved with someone because he cooks a mean sausage."

"There's a lot to be said for a man who can cook," Wiggles said. "I'd be happy if you dated him."

"You'd not only be happy, but you'd also be fat."

"I do not get fat. I burn off excess energy because I run super-hot."

My gaze went to the window again. This was unlike Rhett. If something had come up, it would have been easy for him to send a message to Brogan to let me know he was running late or needed to postpone.

The door opened, and Axel walked in.

"Not him," Wiggles said. "He is not a real man. Promise me you will never date Axel."

Despite my glum mood, I had to smile. For some reason, Wiggles was not a fan of Axel. "He's not so bad. Axel is kind of cute. And as Granny Dottie said, he has loads of money."

Wiggles growled at me. "You date him, and I'm moving out."

"I'll help you pack your bag if you like."

He turned his back on me and stalked out of the cafe. "Tell Brogan I'll have my breakfast out here."

I laughed as I watched him go.

Axel caught my eye and waved. He collected his order from the counter and wandered to my table. "How's everything going?"

"No problems here."

"I heard what happened to Serath and about the arrest Angel Force made. Did you have something to do with that?"

"Not really. I mean, I spoke with Angel Force. I'm not sure about Josh being Serath's killer, but they're convinced."

Axel scrubbed a hand across his chin. "That is a weird one. I went to school with Josh, only pre-school, before the old man shipped me to a fancy boarding school. Josh is a decent guy. A bit of an oaf, but I wouldn't have picked him for a killer. Why did he do it?"

"It's a question to ask Angel Force. They've got him in custody, and no one else can get to him."

"I guess they know what they're doing," Axel said.

"You'd think so, but I sometimes wonder." Angels were beautiful and pulled off wearing white jeans like a super model, but their heads were full of fluffy clouds.

Brogan walked over with our food. He set mine down alongside the pancakes and looked around for Wiggles.

"He's outside," I said. "He's in a bad mood."

Axel grinned. "Let me guess. He doesn't like the company you're keeping?"

I shook my head as I speared a sausage. "Something like that. You'd better avoid him when you leave."

"I'll do my best not to annoy Wiggles any more than required."

"Before you leave, have you seen Puddles' nephew, Dewey, around this morning? She was freaking out earlier because he didn't come home last night. Apparently, he met up with some girl. Puddles is hassling and wants to know where he is."

"Haven't seen him," Axel said. "I'll look out for him today. I wouldn't mind a quiet word after his behavior in your bar."

"That's all sorted. No need to get all macho on my behalf."

"Of course there is. We're friends."

"It doesn't suit you."

"What? Our friendship?"

"No, being macho."

Axel chuckled. "You have a good point."

"I'm sure it's nothing, but you know what Puddles is like when she gets stressed."

"Her face gets as pink as her hair sometimes is." Axel grinned and left me to my enormous breakfast.

After twenty minutes of eating, I felt marginally better about being stood up by Rhett. Still, I did want to know where he was. Partly, it was a pride thing. He needed a damn good explanation for standing me up.

I dismissed the niggle at the back of my head. With Serath dead and Dewey now missing, I needed to reassure myself that everything was fine with Rhett.

If I discovered he'd slept in and forgotten we were meeting, he might also end up in a shallow grave, dug by me.

I paid for breakfast and collected Wiggles from outside the cafe, where he sat next to an empty plate.

"I hope you were nice to Axel when he left."

"I barely noticed the guy," Wiggles said. "Although, I did get an eye-watering whiff of cologne. That could have been him."

"Axel's not so bad."

Wiggles cocked his head. "We both know the reason he's so nice to you."

"He's a friend. That's all. Someone who isn't a friend right now is Rhett. Let's head to his house and see what's up with him."

"You should cut the guy some slack. Rhett is busy leading the notorious Willow Tree Falls biker gang. That's always going to give him a few headaches."

"I'll give him a few headaches if he's forgotten we were supposed to meet."

Rhett lived along a single-track road. His house was a converted warehouse, and he'd done all the work on it himself. I spotted several of his metal sculptures as I headed to the front door. As a sideline, Rhett sculpted incredible creations out of scrap metal. He even had one inside that was supposed to be me.

I hammered at his front door and waited. There were no sounds from the other side. I walked around the back of the house, but everything was locked and shut.

"He could have company," Wiggles said.

Jealousy simmered inside me. "Are you suggesting Rhett forgot our date because of another woman?"

Wiggles raised a paw off the ground and whined. "Forget I said anything. Rhett would never cheat on you."

"He's welcome to cheat on me, since we're not a couple." After staring up at the windows for a few seconds and trying not to picture Rhett in bed with another woman, I turned on my heel. "Let's try the forest. That was the last place we saw him."

After hunting among the trees for an hour, I'd gotten no closer to figuring out where Rhett was. I'd even left a message on his snow globe asking him to contact me and tried not to sound too angry when I did it.

"Tempest!" I turned to see Adin Tombe, one of Rhett's gang members, approach through the trees.

"Hey! I'm looking for Rhett," I said.

"You're not the only one." Adin stopped in front of me. "We figured he was with you."

"He was supposed to be this morning, but he didn't show."

Adin shook his head. "No, I mean we haven't seen him since last night. Someone figured the two of you hooked up and went back to your place."

I shook my head, my anger for Rhett shifting to concern. "There was no hooking up. He's been gone the whole night?"

Adin nodded. "It's not like Rhett to take off without telling anybody what he's up to."

"What is he up to? Is he doing private business he doesn't want anyone to know about?"

Adin shrugged. "He always leaves a message with someone when he goes off just in case a deal goes bad. You definitely haven't seen him?"

"No, we had plans to meet for breakfast and discuss how to help Josh, but Rhett never showed. Where have you looked for him?"

"Everywhere. We've been to the stone circle, the thermal spas, the caves, his house, all the local stores. No one's seen him since yesterday."

Unease ran through me. "Rhett has enemies. You don't think someone's gotten to him, do you?"

Adin snorted. "Rhett knows how to handle himself. If anyone jumped him, they'd be the one with a sore head. It's weird. It's so unlike him."

"This is a dumb question, but you haven't been in touch with Angel Force to see if they've heard anything, have you?"

Adin shook his head and frowned. "We'll make contact as the last resort. We're not keen on them poking around our business."

"I'll make contact. Maybe Rhett's there supporting Josh. He's keen to get him out. He could have put aside his dislike of the angels to speak with Josh."

"I doubt it. But Josh is innocent. No one believes us, but he was with us the night of that guy's murder. It couldn't have been him. Besides, Josh is not into curses."

I nodded. "Rhett mentioned what happened to his mom."

"And Josh has never forgotten it. Even if someone rankled him until his last nerve snapped, he wouldn't use a dark curse like that. He'd be happy to use his fists but nothing twisted like that Serath guy had inflicted on him."

"I'll head to Angel Force and see if they know anything about Rhett. I can also check in on Josh if you'd like."

"Thanks, Tempest. Let me know if you hear anything. We'll keep looking."

"This is strange," I said to Wiggles as we walked away.

"Rhett could be sick. Maybe he's at home but can't get out of bed. He could be desperate for help, running a fever and too weak to move. He could be lying in a pool of his own—"

"Enough! I bet he's fine and got a sniff of a deal and went after it."

"What if he didn't?"

I huffed out a breath. "If Rhett is still missing by the end of the day, I'll get Dazielle to break into his place. And if she won't, I will."

I left Wiggles outside as I walked into the Angel Force headquarters. Sablo looked up from the desk.

"Have you seen anything of Rhett?" I asked her.

"He's not been here," Sablo said.

"Not once? Not even to visit Josh?"

Sablo checked the visitors' log. "There's no signature to show he's been here."

I tugged on the ends of my hair. Where was he? His top priority was helping Josh. Maybe he'd discovered a lead in Serath's murder and had gone after it. But would he have done that without backup from his gang?

"Is Dazielle around?" I asked.

"She's out back."

"I need to see her. This has to do with Serath's murder." I wasn't certain of it, but three missing guys was too much of a coincidence.

I only had to wait a minute before Dazielle sauntered through, an annoyingly smug look on her pretty face.

"Don't tell me you're here to defend Josh's honor."

"I will if I have to, but he's a big boy. He can hang tight until his innocence is proven."

Dazielle arched an eyebrow. "You seem very sure that Josh is innocent."

"I am, but I'm not here about Josh. I'm worried about Rhett. He's also gone missing."

Dazielle pursed her lips. "How long has he been missing?"

"Nobody's seen him since last night."

"That's hardly missing. All that suggests is he had too much to drink last night and is passed out somewhere. Have you tried his house?"

"Yes. We were supposed to meet this morning, and he didn't show. He was the one who insisted on the meeting, so I was surprised when he didn't put in an appearance."

Dazielle grinned at me. "Are you nursing a bruised ego and want to make Rhett pay for standing you up?"

"If I wanted to do that, I wouldn't come here looking for him. I'd sneak up behind him and slam him with a nasty spell."

Dazielle tutted. "I shall pretend I didn't hear that."

I glowered at her. Dazielle was right. I had been angry with Rhett at first, but was beginning to worry, especially after discovering his gang was also trying to find him. "Can you spare a couple of your angels to help look for him?"

"No. Rhett is not missing."

"This is not like him," I said. "It's like he's vanished."

"Tempest, Rhett is a full-grown man. He's more than capable of looking after himself for twelve short hours. Until he's been gone at least seventy-two hours, there's nothing we can do. I said the same thing to Puddles."

"Puddles is looking for Rhett?" This day was getting weirder by the minute.

"No, Puddles came in flapping because her nephew, Dewey, is missing. At least, he didn't come home last night."

"Oh, that's right. I saw her this morning. She barged into my mom's house, stressed out because he didn't show for the meal she cooked him."

"Maybe he went out with Rhett. Are they drinking buddies?"

"I can answer with surety that they are not drinking buddies." I tapped my fingers on the desk. "Don't you think it's weird that Rhett and Dewey went missing on the same night?"

"If they had gone missing, or if someone had seen something dodgy going on that involved them, I'd agree. Just because they didn't make it home last night doesn't mean anything bad has happened."

Something felt off here. First, Serath went missing and turned up dead, then Dewey vanished, and now Rhett. What was going on in Willow Tree Falls?

"You won't help me find Rhett?"

"Come back in two days if he's not made an appearance then we'll talk," Dazielle said.

"You're not a tiny bit concerned, given that other people have gone missing?"

"One person went missing, and we found out what happened to him."

"Yes, he's dead! Murdered by a curse. And you haven't found out who did it," I said.

Dazielle sighed. "Josh is locked up tight in a cell. He's not going to curse anybody else. And he'd never curse Rhett."

"What if it wasn't Josh? What if Dewey and Rhett have been taken by the same person who killed

Serath?"

A flash of concern passed across Dazielle's face before she shook her head. "No, Josh is the man we want. He did it. Just you wait. Rhett and Dewey will turn up full of apologies for worrying everyone."

I turned and stomped away. I was getting nowhere, but Dazielle was wrong. Something odd was going on, and it was up to me to find out just how odd it really was.

Chapter 12

It was late in the day, and I'd spent the afternoon hunting for Rhett and had come up blank. He was nowhere to be found. The last time anyone had seen him was late last night. Since then, there'd been no sign of him. It was as if he'd vanished into thin air.

I'd also asked about Dewey and gotten the same response. Both men had been missing since yesterday.

"My paws hurt," Wiggles said. "We've looked everywhere. We need a break."

I let out a sigh. "I'm all out of ideas about what to do. Where are they hiding?"

"Maybe Dazielle is right and Rhett and Dewey will turn up this evening. You never know. They could have buddied up and headed out of Willow Tree Falls to have some fun."

"Rhett wouldn't do that. He wouldn't leave one of his gang members locked up and head off for fun with Dewey Lavern."

"You'll have to carry me." Wiggles stopped and sat down. "I'm getting blisters."

"You have paws. You don't get blisters."

"I had a pedicure last week. I haven't got much rough skin on my feet."

I eyed him with suspicion. "Please tell me that's a joke."

"A hellhound needs to be in top shape. You never know when an exciting opportunity with a cute furry butt and a winsome wag will pad your way."

"Hellhounds do not get pedicures."

He lifted a paw and whimpered. "My feet hurt."

"I'm not carrying you."

Wiggles lay down and rolled onto his back.

"Stop that. You're making a scene." I looked around as several amused looking people passed by and stared at Wiggles as he whimpered and thrashed around on the ground.

"I'll report you to animal services for cruelty."

"This isn't cruel! You're being a brat."

"I'm your dog. You must help me."

"You're an embarrassment. You can walk. We're just going to Cloven Hoof. I need to make sure everything is fine for tonight. Once we get there, you can have a rest."

"I'm too weak to move." Wiggles continued to roll around on his back and flail his legs in the air.

I walked away a few steps and looked back to see him staring sadly at me.

"You are unbelievable." I walked back, rolled him over, and lifted him onto my shoulder, tucking my hand under his back legs so his front paws could hang over my back.

Wiggles licked my cheek. "I knew you loved me."

I did, but Wiggles took advantage of that. I hefted him higher and strode to Cloven Hoof.

I pushed through the door and into the quiet of my bar.

"Yum! I smell sausages. Let me down." Wiggles wriggled in my grip.

"I thought your feet were too sore to walk."

"I can make it to the kitchen. A sausage will help with the pain." He wriggled again until I let him go, and he raced into the kitchen.

So much for having sore feet. I walked to the bar where Merrie, Izzie, and Blaze were working.

"Is everything good for tonight?" I eased myself onto the seat and gratefully accepted a lemon drop from Merrie.

"As always."

"I don't suppose Rhett's surfaced while I've been away, did he? He should be looking shamefaced and embarrassed about standing me up this morning."

Merrie pursed her lips. "Sorry, I've not seen him. What's he up to?"

"It's a question I'd love answered," I said. "I checked everywhere."

"Have you looked in the forest?" Suki asked as she emerged from the basement, ready for her duties on the door.

"I had a look around this morning. I ran into one of his gang members; that's when I got worried. None of them have seen him since yesterday."

"I can take you back there if you'd like," Suki said. "I know the place like the back of my hand. There are lots of hiding places. I can show you. Rhett might be in one. His gang makes use of those places."

"To do what?"

Suki shuffled her feet. "It's best you don't know. They never caused any bother and were always polite when they spotted me, so I left them to it."

I nodded. I didn't want to know how shady their behavior was. "We need to go before it gets dark."

"We can go now," Suki said. "I need to check in with Fallon, anyway."

I nodded. Fallon was Suki's new assistant, and she'd taken on the role of part-time Forest Guardian ever since Suki had started at Cloven Hoof.

"Hit me with one more lemon drop," I said to Merrie. "And go drag my greedy dog from the kitchen before he eats the entire menu for tonight."

Merrie laughed as she passed me a drink before heading to the kitchen.

Wiggles dashed out a moment later, munching on something stuffed between his jaws.

"Are you ready to keep hunting for Rhett?" I asked him.

He rolled his eyes and shook his head.

"How about I treat you to a steak dinner afterward?"

He tilted his head from side to side before swallowing his mouthful. "You're on. But it needs to be the largest rump steak you have in the kitchen."

"It will be the smallest steak. You look like you've already eaten several plates of dinner. You wobble when you move."

"I was sampling the menu. It's important the chef gets an expert opinion so our customers aren't disappointed."

"You eat anything."

"Some things I turn my nose up at. I'm not overly keen on fruit. And I've never figured out what cauliflower is good for. Well, it's great for one thing. It puffs you up with gas. I can light up the whole street when I—"

"No more talk about your gas issues." I shook my head. "Come on, Suki. Let's go to the forest."

Suki led the way as we entered the forest. She strode confidently along invisible paths as she led us into the deeper parts of the wood.

"There are several small caves around here," she said. "Maybe he's in one of those."

"Why would Rhett be hiding out?"

"Is somebody after him?" Suki asked. "He could be keeping a low profile until the coast is clear."

"I'd wondered that, but he can look after himself. Besides, it's not like Rhett to run from a fight. If someone is after him, he'd stand up to them and chase them out of Willow Tree Falls."

"Halt! Who goes there?" A high-pitched voice bellowed from above our heads.

"It's only me, Fallon," Suki called.

A three-foot, chestnut brown wood nymph hurtled from the branches over our head and landed in a crouched position on the ground. She was dressed in forest-green, her black hair similarly dreadlocked like Suki's. Her sharp black eyes glared at me and Wiggles. "What are you doing in my forest?"

"Now, Fallon, we've talked about avoiding a confrontational tone when you meet people in the forest." Suki's eyes were full of apology as she glanced at me. "Fallon is very good at her job. She's fiercely protective of the trees and everything here."

I smiled, remembering what Suki had been like when we'd first met. She was the same as Fallon when it came to protecting the forest, just a lot bigger.

"That's what I'm here to do." Fallon jammed her fists on her hips. "State your purpose."

"We're looking for someone," Suki said.

"Hey, is that a small pony?" Fallon jabbed a finger at Wiggles.

"I'm no one's pony, short stuff. I'm a hellhound." Wiggles glared at her.

"Oooohhh! A pony who talks." Fallon approached Wiggles cautiously. "Have you got a saddle?"

"Wood nymph, I don't know what your problem is, but you need to look up a picture of a pony." Wiggles took a step closer to me.

"You look like a pony. Well, an ugly pony. Where's your mane?"

"I am not a pony." Wiggles crouched, and his eyes flared red. "Don't even think about riding me."

"Fallon, we need your help," Suki said. "This is Tempest Crypt. She's looking for a friend."

"I know who she is," Fallon said, her gaze still on Wiggles. "She's that witch who has a demon inside her."

I shrugged. "Now we've been formally introduced, I'm looking for Rhett Blackthorn. Have you seen him in here today?"

"Nope, not seen him since yesterday." Fallon clicked her fingers. "Come here, ugly pony."

Wiggles growled and backed away.

"Are you sure?" Suki asked. "Nobody has seen Rhett, and we're worried about him."

"What's to worry about? That guy has moves. He's got serious magic on him. A fallen angel can look after himself."

Although everybody kept telling me that, I needed to make sure Rhett was okay. I needed to look him in the eye and ask him why he thought it was okay to stand me up for breakfast. Not that I was obsessing over that fact, but it was a small issue I needed clearing up.

"When was the last time you saw Rhett?" I asked.

Fallon's button nose scrunched. "He was around when that cursed guy was discovered in the shallow grave."

"That was Serath," Suki said.

"Whatever his name was. Anyway, Rhett was around then. He found the body." She edged toward Wiggles. "I have carrots. Ponies love carrots."

"Fallon, you must focus," Suki said. "We talked about this. You get distracted too easily."

Fallon sighed and stopped stalking Wiggles. "What do you want to know?"

Suki glanced at me and nodded.

"Did you see any unusual activity in the forest last night?" I asked.

"Sure. The forest is full of weird things."

"Something relating to Rhett. What about his biker gang? They were looking for him last night."

"If you mean that group of leather-clad muscle-bound idiots who zoom around on those noisy bikes, then yes, there were plenty of them in the forest last night."

"They were looking for Rhett?"

"That's the name they were yelling out. They searched for hours before giving up."

"But they didn't find him?" Suki asked.

"I reckon not. They were here until the early hours of the morning."

"Anything else?" I asked.

Fallon scrubbed at her chin. "There was someone poking around in the forest. They did not want to be spotted."

"What makes you say that?" Suki asked.

"They used cloaking magic. I got a sniff of them just before midnight. They were skulking around, making noise and digging holes before moving off."

"Did they stay cloaked the whole time they were here?" I asked.

"They did. I followed the sound of footsteps to make sure they weren't causing harm to the forest."

"Were they looking for magical items?" Suki asked. "We bury a number of the important ones to make them harder to find."

"There was no pattern to their search," Fallon said. "It was like they were looking for easy ground to dig."

My heart sped up. "Soft ground that would be easy to dig a large hole in? The sort of hole large enough to put a body in?"

Fallon sniffed. "I reckon so."

"Did you see them dig a big hole?" I asked.

"They might have. I tracked them to the swamp but lost them. It was a good thing they gave up. It was long past my naptime."

"The edge of the swamp is where Serath was found," I said. "Whoever was hidden under that magic could have been looking for somewhere to put another body."

Suki stared at me with large eyes. "You don't think they've got Rhett, do you? They're not trying to hide his body?"

I ignored the panic spiraling through me. "They'd better not have him. Can you take us to the last place you saw this magic user?" I asked Fallon.

"Does a bear poop in the woods?"

"I guess so."

"Wrong! Not in these woods. If I catch any giant furry beast using my forest as their own personal bathroom, I chase them out." Fallon's gaze cut to Wiggles.

"So, you can't take us to the site?" I asked, lost in her riddle.

Fallon tutted. "I can show you on one condition."

"What's that?"

"You let me ride your little pony."

Wiggles bared his teeth. "For the last time, I'm not a pony."

"Let me ride him," Fallon said. "We'll get there much quicker if I do. I've only got little legs, and I tire easily."

I glanced at Wiggles, but the glare on his face warned me not to even suggest he let Fallon ride on his back. "Maybe another time."

Suki rested a hand on Fallon's shoulder. "Show us where you last saw the cloaked magic user. We must ensure the forest remains safe, and they could have been trying to harm it."

Fallon scowled at her. "We can't have that. This way." She stomped away at a surprisingly fast speed, and we all followed her.

"Don't let her anywhere near me," Wiggles grumbled. "I do not like the look in that wood nymph's eyes. She wants to saddle me and whip me like I'm a dumb beast."

"She thinks you're cute," I said. "You should let her ride you."

"I'm nobody's free ride," Wiggles said. "I'm giving myself permission to bite her if she makes any sudden movements in my direction."

"I'm rescinding that permission. Fallon does a good job. You don't want to get on the wrong side of her. She knows where a lot of dangerous magic is hidden."

"If she gets on my back, she'll be on the wrong side of me, and then between my jaws when I take a big bite out of her."

After twenty minutes of walking, we headed across increasingly soft ground.

Fallon slowed and pointed in front of her. "This is the site. I heard them cursing and muttering, so they might have gotten too near and been gifted a boot full of swamp slime. It was after that, that I lost sight of them. They must have given up the hunt."

"Or found exactly what they were looking for. Anyone would be able to dig a hole in this ground." I lifted my black boot out of an inch of soft mud.

Wiggles sniffed the air, and his nose wrinkled. "Although I'm picking up odor of swamp, there's something else around here."

"What can you smell?"

"It smells like that curse Serath had on him when he was discovered."

"Hunt around, Wiggles. Sniff out the source of that smell." I stayed close by him as he stuck his nose to the ground and searched.

It didn't take Wiggles many minutes before he stopped beside a heap of disturbed earth.

"Is this it?"

He backed up and nodded. "It smells worse than the trash when you haven't taken it out for a week. You'll find someone under there."

Fallon grabbed a stick and prodded it into the mud. "Your ugly pony is right. There's something there."

"Scrape back the mud." My heart thundered in my chest. I really didn't want to see Rhett staring up at me.

"Maybe we should call in the angels," Suki said. "I'm not a fan, but they need to know if there's a body in this swamp."

"Let's see what we're dealing with before we get the angels involved," I said. "Go on, Fallon. See what's under there."

Fallon grumbled under her breath, something about not being a slave to some jumped-up witch, as she scraped away the mud.

I peered over her shoulder, and my eyes widened as she revealed a pale hand.

I let out a sigh. "Okay, I've seen enough." I could tell by the manicured nails that it wasn't Rhett.

"Who is it?" Suki whispered.

"I can't be certain, but I think we've found Dewey Lavern."

Chapter 13

It was getting dusk as the angels descended from the sky in a cloud of white feathers and pompous self-righteousness.

Dazielle strode over, her wings ruffling behind her. "What have you got?"

"We haven't uncovered the body, but I'm pretty sure you'll find Dewey Lavern in that mud."

"Puddles' nephew?" Dazielle squinted at the ground, not looking convinced. "He's not back yet?"

"He's not coming back from this," I said. "Can you smell the magic?"

Dazielle sniffed the air and frowned. "It's the same curse."

"Whoever killed Serath also got to Dewey."

Dazielle flapped around as she set her angels to work securing the area. She knelt by the exposed hand and carefully scraped away more mud. It didn't take long before she revealed the frozen, terrified looking face of Dewey.

"You're right." She looked up at me. "How did you know he'd be here?"

"I didn't. I wasn't even looking for him. I'm still on the hunt for Rhett." I glanced at Suki, who stood looking nervous as the angels hurried around her. "Suki suggested we try the forest. We learned that someone had been lurking around last night. We followed the trail, and Wiggles did the rest."

Wiggles lifted his nose. "I'll take payment in fairy cakes."

Dazielle snorted and shook her head, her attention turning to Fallon. "What's your involvement?"

"I tracked the killer as they looked for a place to dispose of the body." She slid a foot toward Wiggles. "We should set up our own crack task force. You can be my faithful pony, hunting out dead bodies, and I will solve the crimes."

Wiggles turned his back and cocked his leg up a tree.

"Fallon and Wiggles the Wonder Pony," Fallon continued. "Solving the crimes the angels have no clue about. We're bound to be busy."

Dazielle glared at Fallon. "Move out of the way and let my team get to work. I want to know everything you saw last night."

"We've already told you what we know." I did not like the accusation lacing through Dazielle's words.

"Tell me again. Who led you here?" Dazielle asked.

I sighed. "Fallon most of the way. Wiggles sniffed out the body."

Dazielle turned on Fallon, who studied Wiggles with an unhealthily obsessive look in her eye. "Why didn't you report this yesterday when you discovered someone in the forest?"

Fallon picked something out of her hair and inspected it. "There are always odd bods skulking around my forest. If I reported them all, you'd spend your whole time in here, and I don't want that."

"What made you suspicious of this particular individual?"

Fallon shrugged. "They used cloaking magic. You don't walk around hidden in this forest without me knowing about it. They were up to something dubious."

"You didn't see them with the body? It wouldn't be easy to transport a body through the forest," Dazielle said.

"They could have come back during my naptime," Fallon said. "A wood nymph needs her beauty sleep. When I lost sight of them, I headed to my dwelling. I had a half-hour nap and continued on my rounds. I wasn't alerted to anything unusual."

Dazielle's shoulders slumped. "This is bad news. We could have a magic using serial killer on our hands. Someone has gotten a liking for using dark curses to bump off their enemies."

"Who did Serath and Dewey have as a common enemy?" I asked. "There must be someone in Willow Tree Falls who hates them enough to do this."

"Is he here?" Puddles bustled through the trees, her blue hair flying out behind her and bright spots of color on her cheeks.

I groaned. "How does she know about this?"

"You know Puddles. She must have seen us flying here and given chase," Dazielle said. She strode over and stopped Puddles from getting too close. "It's best you don't see this."

"Is it my Dewey? Tell me it's not. I knew something dreadful had happened." Puddles clapped her hands on either side of her cheeks as she peered around the trees.

Dazielle tried to lead her away, but Puddles refused to budge. "You don't need to be here. When we have more information, we'll come to speak to you."

"Just tell me, is it Dewey?"

I gritted my teeth. Puddles wasn't going to go until she knew the truth. She did seem to care for her nephew. I felt a bit sorry for Puddles. It was a horrible way to lose a loved one.

I walked over and stood next to Dazielle. "I'm really sorry, Puddles. We've found Dewey."

Tears filled her eyes. "And how is he? Is he hurt?"

"He's not good. Dewey is dead."

Her hand flew to her mouth. "I sensed it in my waters. I knew when he didn't come back last night that someone had gotten to him. How did he die?"

"We're not certain yet," Dazielle said. "We've only just found him. Give us time to investigate, and we can let you have more information."

Puddles dodged past Dazielle. She froze to the spot and gasped when she saw the mud-splattered body of Dewey. Her eyes rolled back in her head, and she fainted.

We both stared at her as she collapsed face down in the mud.

I repressed a sigh. "We need to talk to her," I said to Dazielle. "Puddles might be playing the grieving auntie, but we can't rule out the possibility her dark side has returned. What's to say this isn't an act?"

Dazielle moved back a few steps. "You handle her better than I do. You talk to her."

"She could be a magic using serial killer! I'm not qualified to handle that sort of thing." I also didn't want to babysit Puddles in her current state.

"When she wakes up, take her to Cloven Hoof and talk to her." Dazielle continued to back away. "We'll make it unofficial for now. If she thinks we're suspicious of her involvement, she might shut down and stop talking."

I glowered a Dazielle. She was passing the buck. The blue-haired, hysterical, flapping buck, who never stopped talking unless she was unconscious.

Dazielle raised her hands, palms up. "I'll make it worth your while."

"Hold on. If there's a deal to be made, I need to be involved." Wiggles trotted over. "What are we talking?"

Dazielle pursed her lips. "Fairy cakes for a week?"

I snorted a laugh. "That deal will only work on Wiggles."

"How about I let you off that noise violation from last month?"

I shrugged. "I was planning on protesting, anyway."

Dazielle's wings fluttered behind her. "How about that and fairy cakes for a month?"

"And you take down that unfair sign," Wiggles said.

Dazielle tilted her head. "What sign?"

"The one on your building that says no hellhounds allowed. I'm the only hellhound in Willow Tree Falls. You're persecuting a minority."

Dazielle scowled. "You steal our food, and you break wind all the time. It's not sanitary."

"It's still discrimination. And I can't help it if I have an irritable bowel. My stomach is sensitive."

"You wouldn't have an irritable bowel if you didn't eat so much junk," I said.

"Whose side are you on?" Wiggles asked.

"Yours. Always yours." I looked at Dazielle. "I will handle Puddles if you agree to all of that."

"The other angels won't be happy if the sign goes," Dazielle said.

"Wiggles will do his best not to steal and pass gas, but that's the deal," I said. "Unless you want to escort Puddles home and question her?"

Dazielle licked her lips. "No! Fine, deal made."

"Address the fairy cake order to me at Cloven Hoof," Wiggles said. "I like pink frosting and sprinkles."

Dazielle tutted and turned away.

"Hang on," I said. "With Dewey dead, that means Josh is no longer a suspect. Do you still have him in a cell?"

Dazielle turned back and crossed her arms over her chest. She looked like she wanted to argue, but she didn't have a leg to stand on. "I agree. Josh was there all night. Unless he has an accomplice, he can't be involved."

"You have to let him go."

Dazielle raised her chin. "It could have been Rhett. His disappearance is now looking increasingly suspicious."

"Or worrying. We have two bodies on our hands. Will you now take Rhett's disappearance more seriously, or are you going to wait for another body to turn up?"

Dazielle looked around the trees. "I'll admit it's unusual. I'm still not convinced that Rhett's in any harm."

"You said that about Dewey and look at him. You have to get your angels searching for Rhett. He could be victim number three if we don't hurry."

"We need to assess this crime scene first."

"What's there to assess? Dewey's body is close to the location Serath was found. The magic used feels the same. It's the same killer. Someone is taking these guys, cursing them, and burying them. We have to stop this."

"How is Rhett's disappearance linked to this? It makes sense if someone had a grudge against Serath and Dewey and acted on that. They were friends and could have done something that annoyed an enemy, but they don't run in the same circles as Rhett. Why would Rhett be the next victim?"

As I rubbed my forehead, I grudgingly accepted Dazielle's logic, but I wouldn't be reassured until I saw Rhett and made sure he wasn't lying in a soggy grave with a terrified look on his frozen face.

Puddles groaned and flailed on the ground.

Dazielle swiftly backed away. "If you want to be helpful, get Puddles out of here and talk to her. Where was she last night? Did she argue with Dewey recently? What did she really think of Serath? We need to know all these things before we can move forward."

I gritted my teeth. I didn't want to babysit Puddles, but she could have useful information. I felt torn between staying and trying to find anything that helped in my search for Rhett or dealing with Puddles.

"Where's my Dewey?" Puddles said weakly from her prone position on the ground.

I knelt next to Puddles, still looking at Dazielle. "I'll talk to her. As soon as you know what went on here, you let me know."

"You do the same. If you get suspicious that all is not well with Puddles, don't let her out of your sight."

I helped a bedraggled looking Puddles to her feet. The front of her pastel pink suit was covered in swamp slime, and her hair stuck to one side of her face with an unattractive mesh of green slime.

I picked some slime off her cheek and wiped her face with the sleeve of my jacket. "You've had a shock. Let's get you out of here."

"I can't leave without Dewey."

"Dewey isn't going anywhere. The angels will help him. Come back to Cloven Hoof. Let me give you something for the shock."

Puddles looked down at her clothes and gasped. "I can't let people see me looking like this. I have a reputation in Willow Tree Falls. People won't take me or my business seriously if they see me looking so... so grubby."

"If anyone sees you, they'll understand. It's not uncommon to faint when you get bad news."

"No, absolutely not. I cannot go to Cloven Hoof. I must get changed."

I had nothing in my apartment that would be suitable for Puddles. I liked black, denim, occasionally sparkles, but there were no pastels in my closet. "Let's stop by your house and grab some clothes."

"I need a shower before I can do anything." Puddles fussed over her muddy skirt. "This will need to be dry-cleaned. It's my favorite suit."

It was amazing how quickly she'd forgotten her grief over her dead nephew when she saw her suit was ruined. "Okay, we'll go to yours."

I hurried Puddles away from the crime scene and through the trees, Wiggles walking beside me. As Puddles walked, she muttered to herself and scrubbed ineffectively at the mud, only succeeding in smearing it all over her. I hoped Puddles could hold her sanity together long enough for me to question her.

As we neared the edge of the trees, she slowed and backed into me.

"What's wrong?"

"Check to make sure nobody can see us," Puddles said.

"We can't avoid everybody."

She waved a hand at me, her bottom lip trembling. "I can't let anybody spot me in this state. It's too humiliating."

I peeked out of the trees. "The coast is clear."

She bustled past me, her gaze shooting from side to side as if she expected a crowd to leap out and start taking pictures.

"Quick! Hide!" Puddles squeaked in terror and threw herself behind a hedge as two people approached and walked past.

Wiggles jumped after Puddles. All I could see was his tail wagging and heard the sound of Puddles' startled gasps. I was not sure I wanted to know what was going on behind that bush.

I nodded a greeting to the people and tried to act like it was completely normal for me to be standing by a bush on my own. I waited for them to get out of sight. "Come on. They've gone."

Puddles crept out, her hair tangled with brambles. "Your dog is a menace." She wiped a hand across her cheek.

Wiggles trotted out. "I was being friendly."

"You can't keep dodging people, or it will take hours to get to your place."

"I'll dodge if I like. This is my reputation at stake."

"And my sanity," I muttered.

After two more near misses and two more hedge dives from Puddles, my patience snapped. "This is ridiculous. Grab my arm. I'll use a cloaking spell to get us back to your place."

Puddles' mouth opened. "You'd do that for me?"

"Trust me. I'm not doing it for you." I extended my arm to her.

"I always knew you were a good girl. I never listened to the rumors." Puddles grabbed my elbow as I flung magic over us, concealing us from anybody who walked past.

"What rumors?"

"Oh, you know how people make things up. If ever anyone said anything bad about you, I defended you."

I highly doubted that. Most of the rumors probably came from Puddles, but that was a discussion for another day.

As we entered Puddles' tiny cottage, the smell of lavender hit me. It was like entering a pastel pink, unicorn wonderland. Everything Puddles owned came in a pastel shade. From pale lemon to unicorn blue. She had it all. She also had an inordinate love of doilies. Tiny scraps of lace were dotted everywhere.

"Wait in the living room while I change out of these things." Puddles dashed up the stairs, and I took a few moments wandering around the living room with Wiggles, inspecting the china figurines and unicorn paraphernalia.

I turned to find Wiggles with a piece of lace sticking out of his mouth.

I grabbed it and pulled it out. "Stop that. I know you have a weird fetish about lace but leave the doilies alone."

Wiggles grunted as he looked around the room for something else to chew on. "Puddles has too much lace. It's not the same as chewing a pair of panties, but it's close. She won't miss a few bits. Stuff some in your pocket for later."

"No chance. Sit and be a good boy."

He grumbled to himself as he continued to look around the room.

Puddles returned twenty minutes later, wearing a baby-pink velour lounge suit, her hair bundled in a towel, and a fresh application of lipstick, also in pink.

"Let's talk about what happened," I said.

Her eyes widened, and she nodded as she settled on the edge of her floral couch. "What happened to my Dewey?"

"It looks like the same thing that happened to Serath."

She shook her head. "Who would want to curse my sweet boy?"

"That's what we need to find out and fast. This is the second time it's happened, so the killer could strike again."

Puddles clasped her hands together. "But why Dewey?"

"Puddles, you have to admit Dewey was no angel. He got thrown out of my bar and fought with Serath just before he died. That was in a single night."

"Dewey had nothing to do with Serath's death."

"We know that now."

Puddles slumped in her seat. "I always thought Willow Tree Falls was a safe place."

"It's not that safe. It's full of magic using creatures. Magic is unstable. Power corrupts. Accidents will happen."

Puddles' expression was mournful. "This wasn't an accident."

"You're right, and we're back to square one in figuring out who's involved. Can you think of anyone who has a grudge against Serath and Dewey? Has anyone threatened them recently or come to the house looking for them? What about Bart? Did he fall out with them?"

"Nobody would want to hurt them. They're good boys. And Bart is a sweet boy. They were all friends."

"You said Serath had black magic items in his bag," I said. "Did you not like the idea of Dewey associating with someone who dabbled in the dark arts?"

"Who would like that idea?" Puddles lurched forward in her seat. "Do you think I killed Serath because of that?"

I didn't, not really, but I had to ask. "It could have been an accident. Maybe you got rid of Serath and Dewey found out. Would your darling nephew keep quiet if you'd committed murder?"

Puddles stared at me with her mouth open. She snapped her jaw shut and nodded. "I'll admit I was not keen on Serath, but I would not kill him. He was leading my nephew astray and look where it got him. He's dead."

"Have you still got Serath's bag?"

"Of course. I've yet to return it to his family."

"Can I take a look at what he brought with him?"

"It's in the hall closet." Puddles bustled out and returned with a navy holdall, which she gave to me.

I opened the bag and sifted past the boxer shorts and socks. I lifted out a small book of spells and flicked through it. "These spells are aimed at tourists. Maybe Serath didn't know what he was doing when it came to dark magic."

"It's a slippery path," Puddles said. "You start dabbling in the dark stuff, and things get out of control."

"And you know that how?"

She shot me a glare. "I suspect you know the answer to that. I'm sure Dottie hasn't kept quiet about my past. In my defense, I was a young girl and experimenting. Everyone goes through that phase. I have nothing to be ashamed about. And I promise you this, I do not touch dark magic now."

I sorted through the rest of Serath's things and found a small envelope tucked in the bottom of the bag. I pulled it out and inspected the contents.

"What have you got there?" Puddles asked.

"Old newspaper clippings." I lifted one up. "Do you remember that girl who went missing five years ago, Sandy Bishop?"

"I know a little about her. She was a quiet girl, pretty in her own way. She lived on the edge of the forest with her mother."

"She vanished one day. Nobody found out what happened to her." I stared at the crumpled clipping that detailed her disappearance.

"Some speculated she'd met a young man, and they eloped."

"Her mom left the village not long after. She said she couldn't stay because the memories were too painful. It was weird. There was no trace of anything out of the ordinary, and her things weren't taken."

Puddles nodded. "Why has Serath got clippings about Sandy in his bag?"

"They are about the same age. He might have known Sandy from school. They could have been friends when they were younger."

"Maybe they were sweet on each other, and he hoped he'd find her when he came for his visits. He's here every six months or so, even though he doesn't have family in the village anymore. How romantic."

It might be romantic, but it was also unlikely, given the way Serath behaved around women. "He doesn't strike me as the sensitive type." I tucked the clippings back into the envelope and put it in the bag. This search had gotten me nowhere.

"Going back to Bart, are you sure they were still friends?"

"I'm certain. He's an angel. He's out getting my shopping. If you're looking for someone who is always getting in trouble, what about your boyfriend, Rhett?" Puddles asked.

I narrowed my eyes. "What about him?"

"If it wasn't one of his gang members who killed Serath and Dewey, maybe he's directly involved."

I sighed. I did need to find Rhett and ask that question. "He's missing, the same as Serath and Dewey."

"Is he now? I wonder what he's up to." Puddles sniffed. "It won't be anything good."

"Be careful before you point the finger at other people. You have a lousy alibi for the night of Serath's murder, and I bet you were home alone last night, as well."

"I was until Bart came back. I have a reputation to keep. It doesn't do to be seen out on a work night."

"Your only alibi is yourself again?"

Puddles flapped her hands in the air. "Stop trying to blame me and figure this out. My sister will never forgive me for Dewey's death. She's always considered herself better than me because she married and had a family."

"I'm sure your sister will be devastated about what has happened. This has nothing to do with her being better than you." I tilted my head. Or did it? Was Puddles so jealous of her sister's perfect life that she wanted to mess it up? She decided killing Dewey was the way to achieve that? But a double murder all because you haven't got a husband and two kids? It seemed unlikely.

"She'll find a way to blame me for this, even though I'm innocent," Puddles said.

I stood and handed her Serath's bag. "The angels will be in touch when they have more news about Dewey."

Puddles seemed to have forgotten she should be looking grief-stricken instead of annoyed. She swiftly dabbed at her eyes. "Of course, any news. I must be the first to hear." She walked me to the door.

I nodded goodbye as I left the cottage with Wiggles. I was in need of a long soak in the tub and a good night's sleep after that pastel-themed adventure.

This investigation felt like it wasn't going anywhere fast.

Chapter 14

I wandered into Bite Me for a late breakfast the next morning with Tilly Machello and Wiggles.

Tilly pointed at a table by the window. "I'll be with you in two minutes." She served someone before hurrying over with a plate of breakfast flapjacks and a huge pot of tea.

She grinned as she settled in the seat opposite me, her blue eyes sparkling. "I heard you've had an adventure in the forest."

"Who's been talking?"

"Your Granny Dottie was here yesterday. I can't believe what's going on. Have you got any idea who's throwing curses around?"

I sampled a flapjack. It was still warm from the oven and sweetened with plump raisins. "The angels thought they had someone, but it's not him. I am wondering about Puddles, but the more time I spend with her, the less likely she looks like a real suspect."

Tilly chuckled. "Puddles Lavern, serial curse killer. That's something I can't see happening."

"She still needs to stay on the suspect list. Her only alibi is being home alone when the curses were handed out. She could be putting on a good act."

"Who else have you got in the firing line?" Tilly poured the tea.

I let out a sigh. "Well, with Rhett doing a disappearing act, I am wondering about the gang's involvement."

Tilly arched an eyebrow. "He's in hiding?"

"He might be. We were supposed to have breakfast yesterday, and he didn't show. Even his gang is worried. They've been looking for him, but I've heard nothing from them, so I have to assume he still hasn't shown up."

"He'll have serious making up to do when he does resurface. You don't stand up Tempest Crypt and get away with it."

I nodded, my mouth full of flapjack. I was less angry now and more worried. This was out of character, and with Serath and Dewey dead, I needed to know Rhett was okay.

"Is there anyone else who needs your special investigative attention?" Tilly asked.

"The angels are interested in Izzie."

"You are joking! Why are they interested in Izzie?"

"She dated Serath for about five minutes. They think it's a perfect motive. They consider her a dangerous ex-girlfriend who sought revenge."

"Is Izzie the jealous type?" Tilly said.

"It's not her. I'm sure of it. She was working the late shift the night Serath died."

"Which leaves us with?"

"The only remaining friend who is still alive," I said. "I haven't spoken much to Bart. He was with Serath and Dewey both nights. Although, he claims they separated, so he wasn't around when they were cursed."

"Which seems awfully convenient."

"It does. What's to say they didn't fight? He needs talking to, but I haven't seen him around. He'd better not skip town before I get to quiz him."

"Bart is your prime suspect?"

"I'm not interested in Izzie, and I can't find Rhett to talk to, so he'll have to be."

"Is Bart a magic user?"

"He must be. He got into Cloven Hoof, no problem. I don't know if his magic is up to much, though."

"He needs looking into. Sometimes, people hide how powerful their magic is, especially if they run with the darker spells."

"He wasn't at Puddles' yesterday, or I'd have grilled him then. I'll head to Angel Force and see if they've spoken to him."

"Even if they have, it's worth you doing a second round of interviews. The angels are prone to missing things."

"And pointing the finger at innocent people," I said. "As soon as we finish this plate of flapjacks, I'll get onto it."

Tilly passed around more delicious flapjacks. "How are things with you and Rhett when he's not standing you up?"

"The same as always."

"You mean, he's doing his moody biker act, and you're acting like it doesn't make you hot under the collar?"

"I don't get hot under the collar when it comes to Rhett."

"Okay, so if you're not into Rhett anymore, how about Axel? You're spending a lot of time with him, helping him get over his little problem. Any flickers of romantic lust developing?"

"Nope to any of that. I'm just friends with Axel." I focused on my flapjack.

"Even though he's made it clear he wants to be more than friends?"

"That's his issue to deal with. Axel knew the score when I agreed to help him."

"It wouldn't be so bad if you made a choice about one of them."

"I don't have to make a choice about anything. Axel is a friend, and Rhett's, well, Rhett's in the past. We had a go at a relationship, and it didn't work."

"Because you had your guard up."

"So did he."

"Maybe it's time you both let your guards down. I always thought you two were great together."

"But I'm not into threesomes, and until I get Frank under control, my dating experiences will always be dodgy."

Tilly pursed her lips. "How is my favorite demon?"

"He's being remarkably good. I might finally be getting a handle on him."

"There you go then. You're in control of Frank, which leaves you free to date Rhett."

"I could have my eye on somebody else." I didn't. I hadn't seen anyone in Willow Tree Falls for a while who took my attention. I hated to admit it, but I was still a little hung up on Rhett. If only he didn't look so good in those biker leathers.

"So, date this mystery person. I don't like to think of you alone in the apartment."

"I'm not alone. I have Wiggles."

Wiggles jerked his head up, flakes of flapjack around his mouth. "You kill my love life. I always have to stay home with you and miss out on hot dates."

I gaped at him. "I don't ask you to do that."

"No, but you get that sad look on your face and start walking around wearing big fluffy socks and talking about eating ice cream out of the tub. I know what those signs mean."

"They aren't signs," I grumbled. "I like to be comfortable. And you can go out on dates if you want to."

"Don't worry. I don't miss out," Wiggles said.

"You see," Tilly said. "Even your hellhound is telling you to get a hotter love life."

"I like my love life arctic cold. It makes it easier to handle."

"Sooner or later, you're going to have to make a choice. Rhett and Axel won't wait forever."

"I'm happy to make that choice later." I swiped the last flapjack as I stood. "I'm going to Angel Force to see what they've learned about Dewey's death."

The smile left Tilly's face. "A serial killer in Willow Tree Falls. That's something we do not need."

"You don't need to convince me." I said goodbye and walked out of Bite Me, sharing the last flapjack with Wiggles, who was impatiently waiting outside.

Despite trying to convince myself I didn't care, I was still on the lookout for Rhett. His elusiveness worried me. Why had he gone into hiding? Could he really be involved with Serath and Dewey's murders? If so, why? What had they done that was so bad that Rhett decided he needed to get them out of the way permanently?

Rhett was always straight down the line when it came to murder. He didn't do it. He didn't need to do it. His reputation was enough that trouble avoided him most of the time.

We stopped outside Angel Force. "Hey, look at that. No sign."

Wiggles bounced on his paws. "Dazielle stuck to the deal. I'll be getting my first delivery of pink iced fairy cakes next."

"Let's go see what they know." I walked into the building.

Dazielle was talking to Sablo behind the reception desk. She nodded when she saw me.

"Any news on Dewey?" I asked.

"Nothing surprising," Dazielle said. "It was the same curse that killed Serath, so we have to assume it was the same killer. What did you get out of Puddles yesterday?"

"She's declaring her innocence. Puddles admitted she did not like Serath because he was drawn to dark magic. She was worried he was a bad influence on her nephew."

"She's not got to worry about that now." Dazielle twirled her long blonde plait around her fingers. "And her alibi?"

"Home alone, just as before."

"Which is suspicious."

"It would be if it was out of character, but that's normally what Puddles does. She's a straight-laced woman. She works, then she goes home. She's known for being a homebody. If her alibi had been that she was surrounded by a dozen people, so she had plenty of witnesses, I'd be more suspicious. There's nothing out of character about her being home alone on the nights of the murders."

Dazielle tilted her chin, and an unnerving glint entered her eyes. She couldn't seriously believe Puddles was the prime suspect.

"This is Puddles Lavern," I said, "the lady who likes unicorn colored doilies and tinted hair. Sure, she's a bit annoying, but she's a stickler for the rules. If I'm ever a day late with the rent, she's all over me like a cheap suit. She wouldn't deviate and kill two people."

Dazielle huffed out a breath. "I'm the expert here. You could have overlooked something."

I held my hands up. "You crack her if you can. What about Bart? Have you spoken with him? He's acting evasive."

"I have. He's upset about what happened."

"What's his alibi?"

"He was with Dewey when Serath died."

"Did Dewey confirm that?"

"He did. And he was back at Puddles' when Serath was most likely cursed."

"Most likely? You aren't sure when the curse happened?"

"Curses are difficult magic. We're trying to work out when the curses were placed on the victims. It could have been slow acting magic."

I sighed. "If we don't know when the victims were cursed, how can we confirm their alibis?"

Dazielle arched an eyebrow.

"Fine. You're the experts. I'll leave it to you." I would have liked to explore the curse magic used to see if I could glean anything but was certain Dazielle wouldn't let me near the bodies. "Any news on Rhett?"

"He's still missing?"

"Yes! And since we now have two dead bodies, you need to start looking for him. Unless you want victim number three on your hands."

"If he hasn't shown by the end of the day, I'll consider it," Dazielle said. "Right now, I'm going to talk to Puddles."

"And don't forget Bart," I said. "He needs looking at again."

"He's on the list," Dazielle said.

I headed back to reception. Wiggles was having a standoff with Sablo, who guarded the main door.

"Is everything okay?" I asked.

"I smell doughnuts," Wiggles said.

"You just had a flapjack." I tried to usher him toward the exit.

"He growled at me," Sablo said. "He's not getting through this door. He can come into reception, but that's it."

I shrugged. "A deal's a deal. Dazielle said you can come in. She didn't say how far."

"We need to renegotiate." Wiggles edged toward the main door.

"No! Stay back, or I'll net you," Sablo warned.

"Come on. We need to get to Cloven Hoof."

"For lunch?" Wiggles glanced at me.

"Later, when it's actually lunch time." We had a big party tonight, so it was all hands on deck to make sure it went smoothly.

Wiggles gave one last growl before turning and stamping out the door.

"Your dog is a demon," Sablo said.

I nodded. "Technically, he's a hellhound, but it's close enough."

"He's not getting through to the back," she said. "He can growl at me all he wants."

"I'll tell him that." I hurried after Wiggles. He was a free hellhound, and if there were doughnuts around,

I could never be sure how he'd behave. It was usually badly.

As I entered Cloven Hoof, I saw Blaze busy lining up bottles on the shelf. Merrie had her head buried in paperwork, Ginger was filling the glass shelf, and Izzie was setting out tables.

"While most of you are here," I said, "you should know that Dewey Lavern was found dead last night."

"What happened?" Izzie asked as everyone gathered around me.

"He was cursed, just like Serath." I watched carefully for her reaction. "He was found buried in a shallow grave."

Izzie's face paled, as did everyone else's.

"Someone killed him and hid the evidence?" Merrie asked.

"The angels are working on the theory this could be a slow-acting curse. For all we know, Serath and Dewey were still alive when they were buried."

"How horrible," Izzie said. "Someone must really hate those guys."

"The angels are still looking for the killer."

Izzie's gaze narrowed. "Do they still think I could be involved?"

I had to be honest with Izzie. It was more than likely the angels would be back for more questioning. "The dead guys did hassle you the night they were in Cloven Hoof."

"They hassled a lot of people." Merrie put a protective arm around Izzie's shoulders.

I shrugged. I hated doing this to Izzie. "And you did date Serath."

"I was the one who left him when I found out he cheated. I dodged a bullet."

"You can't be happy that he came back."

Izzie frowned. "I don't imagine many people were happy. That guy was trouble."

"Tempest, you can't think Izzie is involved," Merrie said.

"I don't, but the angels are hunting for suspects, and Izzie is on the list. You need to have your story straight, so they have no reason to come after you."

"My story is straight." Izzie shoved her shoulders back. "I was here, and then I went home. I didn't do it."

"You have no lingering feelings toward Serath?" I asked. "When you saw him at the bar the other night, you felt nothing?"

Izzie sighed. "I wasn't happy. Seeing that smug face dredged up bad memories."

"Were you annoyed enough to wish he was dead?"

"No! Well, maybe once or twice, but that was ages ago. I've moved on." Izzie shifted from foot to foot. "Although, I maybe put a tiny spell on him before he left Cloven Hoof."

"Izzie!" Merrie stared at her. "What did you do?"

"Nothing like a curse," Izzie said swiftly. "I'd never use anything so dark. I was angry when Serath strolled into Cloven Hoof and pretended like nothing bad had happened between us. I thought he was a nice guy and felt like an idiot for being fooled. I decided to teach him a little lesson."

"What magic did you use?" I asked.

"A belching spell. It was supposed to last a couple of weeks. I figured that would put an end to any chances of romance he had while he was here."

I groaned and shook my head. "If the angels get a whiff of this, you'll be in trouble."

"That's why I didn't say anything. I figured they'd find out who killed Serath, and nothing would be traced back to me. I didn't mean any harm. Serath was a jerk. He deserved it."

"He deserved a lot more than a belching spell for upsetting you," Merrie said. "Ginger, why don't you and the others take a break? There's fresh coffee out back and cookies."

Ginger nodded. She caught hold of Izzie's arm and led her away with the rest of the team.

I could tell by the look on Merrie's face she was angry. I hadn't meant to sound like I was accusing Izzie, but she had to be prepared for the angels' ineptitude.

"Tempest, you know we've got a solid team here," Merrie said.

I rubbed my forehead and slumped against the bar. "I know. I'm clutching at straws, but I don't know where to turn next. Josh is innocent because he was behind bars when Dewey was killed. It can't be Puddles, despite her best efforts to look guilty, and I'm not sure Bart is up to the challenge of casting such dark magic. Izzie is a strong magic user. She needs to be prepared when the angels visit."

"She will be. Izzie is a smart young woman. She won't let the angels mess with her." Merrie glanced over her shoulder before continuing. "That's not why I got rid of everybody. There's a problem."

"A dodgy order?"

"The orders are fine. It's Axel. He was being a nuisance last night."

"What was he doing?"

"He came in for a couple of drinks, and everything was fine. As it got later, he started asking the new staff for mushrooms. He knows he's cut off, and he didn't dare ask me. He was flirting heavily with Ginger, trying to twist her arm and get her to slip him some mushrooms."

"She didn't do it, did she?"

"As if you even need to ask. But Axel wouldn't give up. In the end, I stepped in and told him to get lost. I banned him for a month. I hope that's okay."

"He'll get a lifetime ban if he's not careful." I twirled a straw around my fingers. "I thought he was doing well. We meet every week, and he always tells me he's fine."

"Axel's not being honest with you. He seemed uptight and said he'd had a hectic day and needed something to take the edge off."

"If Axel needs to take the edge off, he doesn't do it here. Thanks for handling him. I'll have to keep a better eye on him."

"Don't be too tough on him. Axel is a good guy, and I don't want to see him relapsing."

"I've not been tough enough. He's not taking this seriously."

Merrie tilted her head. "Don't drive Axel away, or he might risk getting his kicks from less reliable sources. He won't know what he's getting if he does that."

"I didn't know you cared." I'd meant it as a joke, but the blush on Merrie's cheeks suggested she might be into Axel.

I was too shocked to say anything else. Merrie Noble and Axel Shadowsoul? I'd never have paired them. I must be reading this wrong.

"He did mention he was lonely." Merrie ducked her head. "You might have to spend more time with him."

"Or maybe I'm not the right person to help," I said. "I'm no expert with this sort of thing. Axel could do with professional help."

"We don't have that kind of specialist in Willow Tree Falls. Most of us have a handle on our magic."

"It could be time Axel takes a holiday and gets some intensive intervention." I felt like I'd let him down. There had been occasions when I hadn't been able to spend enough time with Axel, checking to see if he was doing well. I was distracted with work, my family, Cloven Hoof, Frank, and now these murders. Axel deserved better. He might be a weak-willed idiot at times, but I couldn't see him come to harm.

I looked at the door leading to the back of the club. "I owe Izzie an apology. I didn't mean to make her feel bad."

"She'll understand. A big chocolate cake to make up for it will help."

I nodded. "A big cake will be a start. I'd hate to lose her."

"We've got a great team. We all pull together. She won't take it to heart, and she did use magic against Serath."

"The creep deserved it. I'd have done a lot worse." I straightened up. "Is everything on track for tonight?"

"We've got everything in hand for the party. You focus on finding out who is throwing curses around and make it stop."

"Thanks, Merrie. I can always rely on you." The murders did need to be my focus. Plus, I needed to find Rhett and Axel. Both needed setting to rights, one for messing with my staff and the other for going missing and standing me up. It was time I sorted them out.

Chapter 15

After two hours of looking for Rhett and Axel, without any luck, I headed into Aurora's store with Wiggles.

My eyes narrowed when I saw Toby lounging by the counter, looking like he owned the place.

I took a deep breath and forced a smile. I had promised Aurora I'd make an effort with Toby. Now was the perfect time to show I meant it.

He smiled as he saw me and adjusted the collar of his velvet overcoat. "Another charming Crypt beauty. I hope you're having a lovely day."

"I've had better." I dodged his attempt at kissing my cheek and patted his arm instead.

"Is there something I can help you with?" His gaze locked onto mine, and I felt a second of dizziness.

I stepped back and shivered. Had Toby tried to use magic on me?

"Tempest!" Aurora hurried out from the storeroom at the back. "What are you doing here?"

"Your lovely sister is having problems," Toby said. He side-stepped Wiggles, who was sniffing his pants, and moved behind the counter.

"Missing people," I said, my cautious gaze shifting from Toby. "I've been looking for Rhett for a couple of days and need to have a word with Axel."

"I haven't seen either of them today, but I heard about the second murder," Aurora said.

"You and everyone else in Willow Tree Falls."

"Any idea who it might be?"

"There are a few suspects, but I'm not convinced by any of them. I would like another word with Bart, Dewey, and Serath's buddy, but Dazielle is pulling rank."

"That's not a bad idea to speak to him." Aurora glanced at Toby and looked away. "Especially if the killer is targeting that group. Bart could be the next victim."

I hadn't thought about that. I'd earmarked him as a potential killer, but he could be vulnerable. "It's possible their killer was waiting for them to come back to Willow Tree Falls to get revenge."

Aurora bit her bottom lip. "If that's so, Bart needs to watch his back."

I tilted my head. "Do you know him?"

Aurora looked at the floor. "No, not really."

Her nose had just wrinkled. She was lying to me. "Toby, you asked if you can help. Why don't you get us some cupcakes? I haven't had any lunch yet."

"You ladies deserve something better than cupcakes for lunch." Toby turned to Aurora. "My dear, what would you like?"

Aurora glanced at me. "Actually, cupcakes will be great."

"Your wish is my command." He kissed the back of her hand before leaving the store.

Wiggles watched him go. "You can do so much better."

"Wiggles! Don't be cheeky." Aurora frowned at him. "No more belly rubs if you're nasty to Toby."

Wiggles grunted and vanished behind the counter.

"What gives?" I asked Aurora. "What do you know about Bart?"

"Not much." Aurora looked at the closed door and clasped her hands together. "Oh dear, this is embarrassing, and I didn't want to say anything in front of Toby."

"Don't tell me Bart tried it on with you."

"Absolutely not. Well, I'm not really sure what he tried."

I sucked in a breath. "Aurora, what did he do?"

"I found myself in Puddles' house. I was there with Bart."

My eyes widened. "Found yourself? What were you doing there?"

"That's the thing. I don't remember going there. Bart came to the store and asked for dried silver leaf. I gave it to him, but he didn't leave. He wanted to chat. I didn't mind. I wasn't too busy. Then he asked me out for a drink with him. Of course, I said no. I told him I'm happily involved with Toby."

"But you still went back to Puddles' house with him?"

"No! That's just it. I definitely didn't. At least, I don't remember doing that. All I know for sure is that Bart was friendly and flirting with me, and I was gently giving him the brush off. The rest is hazy. I remember him touching the back of my hand and thinking how cold and slimy his finger felt. My next memory is of me standing halfway up the stairs in Puddles' house. Bart was at the top, beckoning for me to follow him."

My fingers clenched into fists. "That sleazy little magic user. He used something on you, some sort of compulsion spell. He was trying to get you to go back to his room."

Aurora's bottom lip jutted out. "I didn't want to think badly of him, but I came to the same conclusion. His motives seemed less than honorable."

"Less than honorable! He used magic to try to get you into bed. Why didn't you tell me about this?"

"I felt humiliated being duped by him. I can't believe someone would be so underhanded."

"I can believe it with any of Dewey Lavern's friends. Bart didn't hurt you, did he?"

"No, but he got a shock when the magic faded. Bart made an excuse about me being unwell and he thought I'd like a lie down."

"I bet he did." I scowled out the window. "You haven't told anyone about this? Not even Toby?"

"Definitely not. He'd kill Bart if he knew what he'd done. I think Bart used a seduction spell on me." Her hand went to the amber pendant around her neck, and her thumb rubbed across it.

"Rhett's gang mentioned Bart was trying to buy sleazy spells like that when they met in the forest."

"My magic eraser did its job." Aurora always wore a piece of smooth amber set in a silver pendant. She needed something to avoid any side-effects produced by dealing with spells and potions every day.

"I can imagine his disappointment." My shoulders tensed. "He can't get away with this. He could be trying this magic on other women."

"Perhaps he learned his lesson with me," Aurora said. "The next day, he came into the store and was so apologetic. I felt sorry for him."

I snorted. "He was only sorry because he didn't get to have his wicked way with you while you were under the influence of his nasty magic."

"Bart said he had a terrible time finding nice women. He said he knew he'd never stand a chance with someone as lovely as me and promised he only wanted to talk and get to know me better."

"So, he used a seduction spell on you. Good guys don't do that." I shook my head. Aurora was always so quick to forgive and see the good in everyone.

Aurora sighed. "I know it was wrong of him."

"He's not getting away with this," I said. "I'd figured Bart wasn't a strong magic user. Now I'm thinking again. If he's willing to use something as sketchy as a seduction spell, he'd have no boundaries when it comes to using other kinds of magic. That includes dark magic and curses."

"A curse that kills is in a different league to a seduction spell."

"But it shows that Bart has no morals. He uses magic to get what he wants, whether that's a kiss from you or killing his best friends. In fact, Dewey said something about how lousy Bart is when it comes to women. Maybe they teased him one too many times."

"Someone must have given him the curse magic. Bart's magic was weak when he used it on me. That seduction spell wore off quickly."

"Even so, I need to remind him how to treat women." I staggered as Frank's energy curled up my spine. He was as angry as I was about how Bart had manipulated Aurora. For once, I was happy to feed off his anger.

Aurora inhaled sharply and took a step back. "Now, Tempest, there's no need to do anything rash. Bart has apologized. He knows what he did was wrong. Don't let Frank deal with this."

"Maybe that's what Bart needs. A little demon trouble to remind him to be on his best behavior."

"I'd be happy to talk to this feeble magic user." Frank's fury made his words shake in my head. "He dares to touch what belongs to me."

Aurora did not belong to Frank, but now was not the time to have that argument. Frank also had no morals and would be happy to teach Bart a lesson he'd never forget.

The door into the store opened. Toby strolled through with a box in his hands. He froze to the spot and stared at me. "Is something wrong?"

"Toby, quick, get a cupcake and feed it to Tempest." Aurora edged around the counter.

He stared at her as if she'd spoken a different language.

"Quick! It's the only way to calm her demon." Aurora pointed at the box in his hand.

"Oh! Of course!" Toby scrabbled to open the box lid.

"It's too late for cake." I grabbed the box of cupcakes and flung it to the ground before marching out and slamming the door shut, leaving everyone else behind.

Energized by Frank, I ignored Aurora's cries to stop. Normally, Frank would pick hunting Aurora over everything else but not this time. We wanted to hunt Bart and hurt him. He needed educating in how to treat women.

I reached Puddles' front door and slammed my fist against it. I didn't stop thumping until it was opened.

Bart stood there, the annoyed look on his face turning to alarm as I grabbed him around the throat.

"What the—" Bart lost the power to speak as my grip tightened.

I walked him into the house, his feet dangling off the floor, and whacked his head against the wall. "What did you do to my sister?"

"Who's your sister?" Bart gasped.

I growled in his face. "Aurora Crypt. You used magic to get her into this house."

"I didn't," he choked out.

My fingers tightened around his neck. I was so angry I wasn't certain who was in charge. Frank's energy pulsed inside me, but I still had control of my actions. "You're lying."

"Stop shaking me, and I'll tell you what happened."

I released my grip around Bart's throat a fraction. "I'm waiting."

Bart licked his lips, his eyes wide. "I did try to seduce Aurora with magic."

I sneered at him. "Is that the only way you can get a woman?"

"No! Well, maybe. I have trouble getting women to see me in a romantic way. They friend zone me before they've given me a chance."

"It's illegal to use that sort of magic."

Bart shrugged. "She liked me! Aurora was being coy. It's her thing."

I thumped him against the wall again and only stopped when he begged me to. "My sister was not being coy. She's not interested in you."

"I know that now! The magic I used wasn't strong. It wore off before anything happened. I just wanted to spend time with her, so she'd get to know me and realize what a great guy I am."

I snorted in his face. "Good guys don't use magic to get women into bed."

Bart's head sagged. "I'm sorry. Your sister's so cute. And she was being really friendly. I thought I stood a chance with her."

"That's because she is friendly, you idiot. And you need to apologize to her, not me."

"I will. I'll see her tomorrow and make it up to her. I'll buy her something nice, whatever she wants."

My eyes narrowed. "Don't bother. Don't even breathe the same air as her."

"I won't. If that's what you want. I'm leaving Willow Tree Falls tomorrow, anyway. I won't be back. I only came to visit because Dewey twisted my arm."

I sucked in a deep breath and pushed Frank back a fraction. Now I had Bart by the throat, I could question him about the murders. "Not so fast. You've got some explaining to do."

"About what?"

"Two dead friends."

"Oh! Well, it sucks. They were cool guys." Bart pointed at my hand that was still clamped on his neck. "Any chance you can let me go?"

"No. Where were you on the nights they died?"

His brow wrinkled. "I already told the angels this."

"Tell me."

"I was with Dewey, sleeping in a crypt the first night. I was with Puddles when Dewey went missing."

"You could have cursed Dewey and then returned to Puddles' house."

Bart shook his head. "As your sister has experienced, my magic is lame. I can't even keep a simple seduction spell active for more than a few minutes."

"You could be concealing stronger abilities."

"I've always been lousy at magic. My mom, who's a witch, married a human. I got half her ability, and she isn't a powerful witch. I tend not to bother with magic much. It's easier to blend in when I'm in the outside world if I'm not flicking magic around all the time."

I had to admit I didn't get a sense I was dealing with anyone with great power. "Tell me about your meeting with Rhett's gang."

Bart blinked at me. "The biker gang?"

"They told me you've been skulking around the forest."

"If you let go of my neck and stop smacking my head against the wall, I'll tell you everything."

I took a step back, Frank's energy still boiling inside me, desperate to leak out and pound this piece of dirt into the ground. I needed to get better control of him, or this could turn into a mess I'd have trouble explaining.

"It was Dewey's idea," Bart said. "He was bragging that he knew the local biker gang and they were friends."

"You decided to see if that was true?"

Bart nodded. "Dewey reckoned they wanted him to join, but he kept turning them down. We insisted we meet them and find out if it was true. At first, Dewey didn't want to take us, but when we challenged him, he caved in. He dragged us into those woods."

"What happened?"

"We met a gang member; in fact, we met several." Bart rolled his shoulders. "They weren't interested in Dewey. They laughed in his face and treated him like a joke."

"Yet you still bought produce from them?"

Bart scratched his head. "We didn't have much choice. They got a bit rough. To calm things down, I said I'd buy their supplies. It worked. They were happy enough to take our money. But they cheated us. What they gave us didn't work. We ate the whole batch and didn't feel anything."

"Did any of the gang members hurt you?"

"They were threatening to but didn't follow through. Why, do you think they're involved with killing Serath and Dewey?"

"I'm more interested in you right now," I said. "Don't leave Willow Tree Falls until this investigation is over."

"You don't think I'm a suspect, do you?" Bart's laugh was startled. "My magic is rubbish, and I have alibis for both nights."

"You knew the two victims, and you were with both of them the nights they died."

"That's not true. Serath stomped off in a rage after we teased him because that cute barmaid shut him down. I wasn't with Dewey when he died. He went off with a woman. I don't know what happened after that."

I nodded as I remembered hearing about Dewey's hot mystery date. "Who did Dewey meet that night?"

"I don't know who she was. The whole thing was weird. We went out to grab something to eat, then went for a few drinks at the Ancient Imp. Dewey went to the bathroom and was gone for ages. When he came back, he was acting strangely. His eyes were glazed over, and he kept muttering to himself. I thought he'd had too much to drink. Then he said he had to go and walked out of the bar, leaving half an ale and me standing alone."

"Where did he go?"

"I tried to follow, but he told me to stay where I was." Bart stuffed his hands into his pants pockets. "I went outside anyway and saw him wandering toward the forest. He was wasted, staggering from side to side. It was funny to watch. There was someone waiting for him. I'm sure it was a woman, but she had a hood pulled over her head, so I couldn't see her face. I saw long hair poking out the sides. Dewey met her, and they walked into the woods together. I figured he'd gotten lucky and was taking her off for some fun."

"You didn't see her face at all?"

"No. It was dark, and she was a long way away. She was short, though. She only came up to Dewey's shoulder."

"What was the color of her hair?"

"Not blonde, but that's all I can tell you. That was the last time I saw Dewey. I decided not to follow him. I'm not some pervert who watches his friends make out with a girl."

"No, you're just a pervert who uses dodgy magic to get women into your bedroom."

Bart muttered under his breath and scuffed a foot on the floor. "I said I was sorry."

This left me with a puzzle. There were no women in Rhett's biker gang, so it made it unlikely that whoever killed Dewey had a link with them. Puddles and Izzie fit the female criteria, but I couldn't imagine Puddles stooping to wearing a hoodie. If she did, it would be lemon-yellow or sky-blue. That left Izzie. My gut tightened. She owned several hoodies.

"I promise you I had nothing to do with either of their deaths. I'll admit to messing with your sister, but that's it."

I glared at Bart. "Don't do it again. Not with anybody."

"I only did it because that's what Dewey and Serath do when they like someone."

"They've used seduction magic to get women?" My blood boiled again, and Frank's energy reared up. Maybe I shouldn't waste my time investigating their deaths. It wasn't a bad thing that someone had gotten rid of them.

"They said it's easier than having to go on dozens of dates and spend loads of money before the girl decides she doesn't like you and you've wasted your time."

My fist slammed against the wall, right by Bart's ear. "You need to rethink your seduction techniques.

No more magic."

The sound of running feet had me turning. Dazielle raced to the door, closely followed by Wiggles. "Tempest, you're here! We had a report of a fight at this address."

"There's no fight here, is there?" I glared at Bart.

He swallowed loudly. "No, sure. Everything is fine. We were having a chat. Real friendly, like."

"You'll have to finish your friendly chat later," Dazielle said. "There's a problem."

"What's wrong?" I asked.

"We think Axel's been taken. He's the curse killer's next victim."

Chapter 16

I left a startled looking Bart and raced out of the cottage with Dazielle. "Why do you think Axel's been targeted by the killer?"

"We've been trying to find him since this morning," Dazielle said. "I sent an angel to his house regarding a complaint of lewd behavior."

"What did he do?"

Dazielle grimaced. "Nothing pretty. There was no answer at his place. When Sablo looked through a ground-floor window, she noticed furniture knocked over and signs of a fight. We think he's been abducted."

My heart raced as we sped along the street. Axel gone, as well. This was not a coincidence.

"What about Rhett?"

Dazielle nodded. "I've dispatched an angel to his home to see if there are signs of an attack."

At last, the angels were taking this seriously. It only took the abduction of a wealthy, well-connected half-demon to spur them into action.

Wiggles nudged me with his nose. "Is everything good?"

I shot him an apologetic look. "Sorry for leaving you behind. Frank wanted to teach Bart a lesson regarding his treatment of Aurora."

"Did it work?"

"Bart won't be seducing women with magic ever again."

Wiggles nodded. "That's all that matters, and I got a chance to eat all the dropped cupcakes in Heaven's Door. They were delicious."

We arrived at Axel's house. Two angels stood outside the front door. We walked in, and Dazielle nodded at an angel inside who was taking pictures and bagging evidence.

"You see, overturned chairs and things pushed out of the way." Dazielle gestured around the lounge.

I nodded as I walked slowly around the room and into the kitchen.

Dazielle followed me. "Any idea who'd want to get even with Axel?"

I shook my head. "There are two coffee mugs here. Why would Axel make coffee for his attacker?"

"He must know them," Dazielle said.

"Were there signs of a break-in?"

"No, the windows are secure, and there's no sign of tampering on the door locks."

"Which means Axel let the person in, made them coffee, and they jumped him. He fought back in the lounge but wasn't strong enough to stop whoever it was from taking him."

"Axel must be connected to Serath and Dewey if this is the same person," Dazielle said. "Do they know each other?"

"He recognized Dewey in Cloven Hoof the first night he arrived, but he doesn't know him well." My gaze settled on a small brown paper bag, and I frowned. As I suspected when I looked inside, there were dried mushrooms in there. Mushrooms that came from Cloven Hoof. Axel had lied to me. He was still using mushrooms. How had he gotten his hands on supplies from my bar? Everyone knew not to serve him.

"The coffee in these mugs is tepid," Dazielle said. "Whatever happened here, it wasn't long ago. I'd say less than an hour."

"Which means Axel is still alive," I said.

Dazielle nodded. "The curse takes time to work. We think our killer curses his victims, so they can't move but are conscious and aware of what's going on. They then bury them and leave them to die. It's a horrible way to kill a person. They'd know everything that was going on but can do nothing to stop it from happening."

I shuddered. This person had to be stopped. "When I was... chatting to Bart, he revealed that he saw Dewey heading into the forest with a woman. He didn't have much of a description, but I think we're looking for a female magic user."

"And a strong one," Dazielle said. "There are plenty of those in Willow Tree Falls. You're one."

I scowled at her. "Check my alibis if you like. This has nothing to do with me."

"Maybe it's a man hater," Dazielle said. "She could target guys she's taken a disliking to."

I tapped my finger against my lips. "You might be on to something. It could have to do with the way these guys treat women. I saw Dewey and Serath in action at Cloven Hoof. They were hassling my bar staff and being disrespectful. Bart's admitted they've all used seduction magic to get women they want."

Dazielle's nose wrinkled. "I'll be having words with Bart. Some time in a cell will convince him to learn new manners."

"Frank and I have already spoken to him, but it's worth shaking him down before he leaves."

Dazielle nodded. "Where are you going with this theory of our curse killer targeting arrogant guys?"

"Axel is known for flirting with anyone even mildly attractive. Most of us are used to him, but if he met someone new and offended her, he could have gone on her hit list. She's targeting guys who don't treat women well."

"It's possible. Whoever it is, we don't have much time to find her and stop her from killing Axel."

My head pounded. "How long have we got?"

"Forty-eight hours, if that. From our tests of the magic used that's how long it takes before the curse fades."

"Let's go find Axel." I headed to the door, Wiggles by my side.

"Where are you going?"

"Into the forest, near the swamp. That's where Serath and Dewey were found."

"We'll catch up with you," Dazielle called. "We need to finish with this crime scene."

I waved a hand to let her know I'd heard. Angels moved a lot faster than I did. The wings were a bonus if you discounted all the shedding.

"I'm not keen on Axel, but even I don't want to see him cursed and buried alive," Wiggles said as he munched on something he'd most likely stolen from Axel's trash.

"Same here. We need to start in the forest. Maybe the killer takes them there and spends a few hours terrifying them before shoving them in the ground."

"I don't want to worry you," Wiggles said as he ran alongside me, "but Rhett is still missing. And he's been gone longer than Axel."

"I haven't forgotten," I said. "The problem is, is Rhett missing because he's involved in these killings or because he's also been taken by the curse killer?"

"If Rhett is involved in killing Dewey and Serath, would he use somebody to get to them?"

"Like a honey trap? You think he's got a witch on his books helping take these guys out?" That didn't sound like Rhett. If he had business to deal with, he did it himself and didn't hide behind others.

Five minutes later, two angels shot over my head, heading in the direction of the forest.

"We'll meet you there," Dazielle yelled from above me.

I nodded as I continued to run. What I wouldn't do for a pair of giant wings right about now. Or just a decent pair of running sneakers.

We got to the edge of the forest, and I slowed, taking in a few deep breaths. Although the forest wasn't huge, it was dense and difficult to navigate.

"Let's start at the swamp," I said to Wiggles.

Wiggles bounded ahead, his nose to the ground.

I spotted Dazielle and Sablo up ahead and ran to join them.

Dazielle nodded at me. "We'll move the search out from the edges of the swamp. We can flush our killer out if she's in hiding. We must be careful. If she becomes aware we're onto her, she could panic and abandon Axel. We need to find out where she's stashed him."

"If she does panic, she might kill him to get the job done quickly," I muttered.

Four more angels joined us, and we spread in a long line as we reached the swamp.

I tried to keep my focus, but inside I was panicking. This was too close to home. Whoever this killer was, they were targeting people I cared about, and I couldn't let that happen.

We'd been searching for half an hour when I heard breaking twigs underfoot and muttered conversation. I stopped walking and stared through the trees. Was the killer walking toward me?

Slowly, one by one, members of Rhett's gang appeared. None of them looked happy to see me or the angels.

"Hey, guys." I did not like the angry glint in their eyes. "Is there a problem?"

Ian Blaine stepped forward, his top lip curled. "You're the problem. You and the angels need to get out of our forest."

"We're not looking for trouble," I said.

"Then what are you doing here?" Ian drew closer, his fists clenched by his sides.

"Probably the same as you," I said cautiously.

His eyes narrowed. "You've no business being here."

"You don't own this forest," Dazielle said. "We're on official Angel Force business."

"You can stick your official business."

Dazielle's wings fluttered. "I won't hesitate to have you arrested if you stand in our way."

I pressed my lips together. Dazielle made us sound like nosy, irritating officials. "We're looking for someone. They could be hurt."

"So are we." Ian took a step closer. "Who are you looking for?"

"Axel Shadowsoul. We think the curse killer has taken him."

Ian snorted. "We don't care about some jumped-up trust fund half-demon. We're looking for Rhett. You need to get out of our way. Rhett doesn't like snooty angels or stuck up witches involved with his business."

"That's not going to happen," Dazielle said.

The gang moved forward in a single wave of menace. The angels didn't back down. Instead, they spread their wings, tension radiating off them.

As entertaining as it would be to see the angels and the gang go toe to toe, I did not have time to watch a fight.

"Stop!" I stood between the angels and the biker gang. "This magic user doesn't mess around. They killed Serath and Dewey and could be about to do the same to Axel. And, since Rhett is missing, it's possible that the curse killer has him, as well."

Ian licked his lips, his gaze darting to the side. "What makes you say that?"

"Tempest, do not share confidential information with a bunch of criminals," Dazielle muttered.

I ignored her. "There's evidence at Axel's house of a struggle before he vanished."

The gang exchanged glances.

Ian looked around the group before nodding. "We found the same thing at Rhett's place. There was blood on the floor and things kicked over."

My heart thudded in my chest. "Who has Rhett annoyed recently?"

"I'll give you a long list." Ian's lips thinned.

"The killer can't have Axel and Rhett at the same time," Dazielle said. "The magic would be too difficult to contain. They'd lose control."

"She must be a strong magic user," I said. "She could have incapacitated one of them while she kills the other."

"She?" Ian said. "You know who this is?"

I waved a hand at him. "No, no details. But the killer was seen with Dewey just before he died."

"Rhett's not stupid. He wouldn't go off in the forest with some strange chick, even if she is cute."

"We also believe Axel knew her, so maybe Rhett also recognized her. He wouldn't be suspicious of a friendly face."

"How long has Rhett been missing?" Dazielle asked.

"Two days," Ian said.

"What's the connection?" Dazielle asked. "How does Rhett know Dewey and Serath?"

Ian scrubbed his chin. "He wouldn't waste time on those losers."

I shook my head. "We don't have time to figure out the connection. Axel and Rhett are out here somewhere. We have to find them before it's too late."

The gang and the angels glowered at each other for a moment, no one willing to concede.

"Come on! This is a matter of life and death. With more of us, we can cover a bigger area of the forest more quickly."

Dazielle nodded. "We can work together, but I'm in charge."

"You can think that if you like, Feathers," Ian said. "You don't call the shots when it comes to what we do."

I gritted my teeth. "I don't care who's in charge, but we have to find them. Now!"

"Conducting a search is my area of expertise," Dazielle said. "If nobody takes the lead, it will be a mess. We will miss vital information."

I listened to the gang and the angels bicker about who should be in charge, my frustration growing. This was a nightmare. They seemed more concerned with pulling rank than finding Rhett and Axel.

I needed help from someone who didn't have a stake in this. Someone who had enough power to take on a dangerous curse killer and survive. I hated to admit it, but I needed Frank.

I stepped away from the bickering group and snuck behind a tree.

"That look on your face is giving me the chills," Wiggles said.

"I bet it is. We need an extra hand."

Wiggles cocked his head. "You're going to bring Frank in on this?"

"He'll sense the dark magic. Frank might even know who's behind this. Anyone who's using magic this dark has to have some demon in them."

Wiggles backed up a step. "Can you control him once he's out?"

"Probably not, but it's our only option." I gestured to the bickering group. "They're intent on attacking each other rather than focusing on the real problem. By the time they figure out who's the boss and how to conduct a search, it will be too late. We don't know how long Axel and Rhett have been cursed or the strength of the magic used on them. We could already be too late to save Rhett." I swallowed against the tightness in my throat. We could be standing here arguing and they could already be gone.

I couldn't think about that now. I had to believe there was still time for Rhett and Axel.

I took a deep breath and looked down at Wiggles. "You might want to get out of here."

"No way. I'm sticking by your side, even when Frank's got control of you. If he gets too much, I'll bite his leg."

"That will only anger Frank and hurt me."

"I'm still staying," Wiggles said.

I was glad to have his company, even though it was a risk him remaining here when Frank was in charge.

"Frank, any chance you want to come out and play?" His warm energy curled over me as if he was stretching from a deep sleep.

"A rare invitation to get free in Willow Tree Falls. What do I owe the pleasure?"

"We have to stop someone using curses to kill people," I said. "If I let you out, can you get a fix on the magic being used?"

"Of course. The real question you need to ask me is if I want to come out and help."

"I've no time for games. Do you want to get free or don't you?"

Frank chuckled as his energy wove up my spine, tickling the back of my neck but going no further. "How about we make a deal?"

I gritted my teeth. "I'm not making any deals with you."

"If I agree to help, I want a weekend away with me in charge. You won't get an opportunity to surface for two whole days and nights. I choose the venue. I choose what we do."

I scowled, hating the idea of not being in control for forty-eight hours. "No killing."

"When have I ever killed?"

"Plenty of times."

"Never when I've been with you. I may partake in a little gentle maiming, and a few limbs have been lost, but my playthings always survive."

"No killing and no maiming. And I do not want to wake up in some stranger's bed because you took a fancy to them."

"A demon has to have some fun. Not even a little debauchery?"

"No debauchery."

"I'm not sure that's a good enough deal. It's almost as if you don't want your friends to survive."

I knew Frank had been listening the whole time. "You'll get your weekend away, and right now, you get the chance to get loose in Willow Tree Falls." That was a carrot he could never resist.

He purred in my head. "I can pay your sister a visit. I've been meaning to have a one-on-one chat with that boyfriend of hers. I do not like that goatee."

"You and me both, but we can't worry about Toby's facial hair. We've got a killer to locate. Do we have a deal?"

"We do. I'll ensure we find this killer and destroy him."

"No destruction. And our killer is a woman."

"Even better. Some of the darkest magic users are women. It's to do with how bitter they get following a betrayal. Their magic becomes twisted and sly. Curse-using females are a delight to be around. I'm surprised there aren't more female demons in the world."

"Let's discuss the male to female demon ratio another time." I dropped my barriers. "Over to you, Frank. Do your worst."

"I always do." His hot energy flooded over my head.

I blinked as the world turned red. I stretched, yawning loudly as I stepped around the tree and saw the angels and biker gang still feuding.

I shook my head and left them to it. Those petty idiots could fight all they wanted. They'd only slow me down.

Although Frank was in control, I wasn't fighting him this time, so it was easier for us to talk.

"Can you sense anything? The bodies of Serath and Dewey were found by the swamp. It's likely Axel and Rhett are also here."

"I am sensing dark magic." Frank propelled me through the forest, Wiggles close to my side.

"How is my little hellhound? Have you missed me?" Frank asked.

"Can't say I have. Although you do have a great gift for hunting out the best food when you're in charge of Tempest."

"We have that in common." Frank paused and sniffed the air. "This way." We turned and headed deeper into the forest.

The sounds of the arguing angels and bikers disappeared as the trees closed in around us.

"There's an unpleasant, sticky residue in the air," Frank said. "It's like a spider web. You track one thread, and it will lead you to the center of the magic." He changed direction several times, stopping, sniffing and then moving on.

"What are you doing? Don't mess me around. My friends' lives are at stake."

"I'm not messing around," Frank muttered. "There's a lot of dark magic here. It's muddled with the energy of the forest."

"There's more than one person using curses?"

"No. There are two different locations where a curse has recently been used. The energy emanates from both of them. I'm being pulled in opposite directions."

"You must be picking up on the curses placed on Axel and Rhett."

"Then you have a problem," Frank said. "The locations are on opposite sides of the swamp."

"Can you get an exact location?"

"I can. The magic was placed at different times but is reacting at different speeds."

"Rhett would have been cursed first."

"I feel a curse that is well-established on one person."

"Then we go get him first," I said.

"As you wish, but the other individual's curse is almost complete, as well."

The worry throbbing through me pushed against Frank's power. "How is that possible if the curse was placed on them at different times?"

"We must have disturbed the killer. They altered their magic to ensure Rhett and Axel perish before they are found. The activation of a curse can be adjusted."

"How long have we got?"

"Within the next ten minutes, they will both be dead."

I struggled to breathe as my emotions overwhelmed Frank, leaving me free for a moment. My mind whirled with horror.

"What are you going to do?" Wiggles asked. "You can't save them both."

"You make an excellent point, my hellhound," Frank said as his energy slid back over me, and he took control again. "Who do you want to save, Tempest, Axel or Rhett?"

Chapter 17

Despite Frank being in charge, I still felt panic throbbing inside me. I didn't want to choose between Rhett and Axel. Whatever decision I made, a friend would die.

"We'll go back and get the angels," I said.

"We're not involving those buffoons," Frank said, forcing me to remain on the spot. "When they realize I'm in charge, they won't pay attention. They will probably attack."

"The gang then," I said. "They won't care if I'm controlled by a demon."

"By the time you go back and lead them to the bodies, the curse will be complete, and your friends will be dead. You will have lost them both."

I was glad Frank had control of my body; otherwise, my knees would be shaking. "Where is Axel?"

"He's closest to us. I sense his half-demon ability. Rhett is on the opposite side of the swamp. His power has a different flavor."

I had no way to send a message to Dazielle to let her know what was going on and direct her to one of the victims. There was no one who could help.

"Tempest, you're at a crossroads. You must make your decision. Who do you want to save?" Frank sounded like he was enjoying this.

"I want to save both of them." It wasn't fair. What did the curse killer want with Axel and Rhett?

"If you do not decide, I will make the decision. Perhaps I will choose to save neither and go play with your sister instead."

"No! You made a deal with me."

"Then make your choice. Your anxiety is making me sweat."

I looked down at Wiggles. "Who would you choose?"

"You need to ask? Axel is a jerk."

"He's not a jerk who deserves to die."

"Rhett is your guy. He's on the shady side, but he's generally sound."

"But Axel is vulnerable and alone. Rhett has his gang to look out for him."

"Axel is a trust fund baby. He has all the luxuries a half-demon desires. He wants for nothing."

I groaned. "Fine. I've made my decision. I choose Rhett."

"I am disappointed," Frank said. "I always favor the demons. Fallen angels are so intense and emotional."

"Where is Axel?" I asked.

"You'll find his body two miles east of the broken bridge leading out of Willow Tree Falls," Frank said.

"I'll tell the angels." Wiggles raced away, his tiny legs a blur as he shot through the trees.

"Let's rescue Rhett," I said. "Don't be slow about it."

My head jerked back as Frank blasted into action. Demons can move fast when motivated. My heart felt like it would burst out of my chest as he flew past trees and bounded over rocks.

"We're almost out of time," Frank cautioned. "Your dithering could have killed him."

"Keep going."

"You're overheating. I can sense it."

"It doesn't matter. Don't slow down."

Frank grunted and pushed on. The ground underfoot grew damp, and we soon squelched through ankle high muck.

"This can't be the place," I said. "It's too swampy. You can't bury a body here."

"But you can here." Frank made a huge leap, grabbed hold of a tree and swung around it. We landed on the other side, my knees protesting as I thudded to the ground.

"Where is Rhett?"

"Under this mound of earth." Frank was on the move again before I was dropped to the ground beside a pile of recently turned mud.

I shoveled sticky, foul smelling mud behind me as Frank's energy ebbed back, and I felt my control slip back into place.

"I should warn you, Axel is about to perish. He only has a moment of air left."

I blinked tears out of my eyes. "Frank, please, is there anything you can do to save him? Are the angels on their way?"

"Our hellhound has just reached them. They don't believe what he's saying. It appears they have trust issues when it comes to Wiggles. By the time he convinces them, it will be too late, and your friend will be dead."

"Axel can't die." I dug faster. If I could get Rhett out quickly, maybe I could get back to Axel.

"You've made your decision. You picked Rhett."

I flung mud in all directions, using my arms as scoops, despite the muscles burning with the effort. "There must be something you can do. You're a powerful demon."

"I am that." He was silent for a second. "Perhaps for another weekend in control of what we do."

"You are a hateful demon," I growled. "You're bargaining when a person is dying."

"As you just said, I'm a demon. My morals are on the wonky side."

"What morals?"

Frank chuckled. "The same conditions. I promise not to debauch, kill, or maim too badly. One more weekend, and I will help Axel."

I had no time to negotiate. "Do it. Anything to save him."

"As you wish."

I struck something warm. I slowed my frantic digging as I discovered a hand underneath the mud. I slid my hands up and dug carefully until I revealed Rhett's face.

A sob choked out of me. "He looks dead."

"He's very close to death, but he's still breathing," Frank said.

"Give me back full control," I said. "I can use my magic to heal him."

"Make sure you keep your promise. And be careful. What I have summoned to assist Axel will not go quietly. One false move, and it will be your funeral everyone is attending."

I continued to scrape mud from Rhett's eyes and mouth as Frank's power faded. "What did you summon?"

"You told me to do anything, and that's what I've done. I hope you can live with the consequences." Frank's energy slid down my spine, and I no longer heard him in my head.

I leaned over Rhett and let out a relieved sigh when I heard quiet breaths coming out of him. I pressed my hands against his chest and pumped him full of healing magic, focusing on connecting with the power of nature around us and filling him with life.

As I touched Rhett, I felt the sticky residue of dark curse flicker across my skin.

The curse was fading. The magic had achieved what it needed to do. The curse killer must assume Rhett had suffocated as he was held in place by the dark magic.

Rhett's eyes flickered open, and he sucked in a huge breath.

I kept my hands pressed to his chest, keeping the magic flowing until color returned to his cheeks.

His eyes struggled to focus, but his gaze finally locked with mine. "Tempest?"

"I'm here. The curse didn't get you. Lie still. You've taken quite a magical beating."

"It isn't safe." He coughed, and his eyes closed again.

I shook my head. "Don't worry about anything. The magic user isn't around."

"You're not hurt?" His voice sounded hoarse.

"No, I'm fine. I got here in time. Everything will be okay."

"Your bar!" His eyes blinked open, panic clear in his dazed expression.

"Cloven Hoof? What about it?"

"It's dangerous."

My brows lowered. My bar wasn't dangerous. Other than the occasional crazy night, it was one of the safest places to be. "I don't understand."

Rhett faded for a moment before gasping in a breath. "The curse killer is in your bar."

My heart stuttered in my chest. "Are you talking about Izzie?"

Rhett coughed again, and his eyes fluttered closed, his head dropping to the side.

I checked his pulse, which was strong and regular. It seemed that the effort of talking had knocked him out.

I sat back on my heels and tried to puzzle through what he meant. Was he warning me that Izzie was dangerous?

My gut twisted, and my vision went blurry. Had I made a huge mistake? Had I overlooked the real killer because she was a friend?

The smell of sulfurous gas filled the air, followed by an ear-piercing explosion that rocked the ground beneath me.

I recalled Frank's words about watching my back when help arrived for Axel. What or who had Frank summoned?

Another explosion filled the air, and I saw a spray of fire blast through the treetops.

I did one final check on Rhett. He seemed stable, and there was nothing more I could do to help him right now.

I raced away. I had to find out what was going on. What had Frank done to keep Axel safe? Maybe the bargain I'd made to save him would be too high of a price to pay.

Chapter 18

I sped toward the site of the explosion. As I grew nearer, my pulse raced. The angels and the biker gang had joined forces and faced down a ten-foot mass of writhing red smoke.

As the smoke solidified, long twisted horns, talons, and a bulky flame-red giant of a demon stepped forward.

I slowed, and my eyes bugged. What was most amazing about this scene was that Axel lay on the ground, covered in sticky mud, and the demon appeared to be protecting him.

An angel screamed as the demon threw her against a tree before lunging at Dazielle.

Dazielle's wings were fully extended, and she hovered three feet off the ground to match the height of the demon.

"This is help?" I muttered to Frank.

Frank chuckled. "I knew he would come to assist in this little problem."

"Why? Who is he?" I flinched as a gout of flames shot from the demon's mouth.

"Don't you see the family resemblance? That's Axel's father."

"That's Kroni!" My jaw dropped, and my mouth went dry. Of course, it made sense. He'd want to protect his son when he realized he was in mortal danger. My brain froze for a second. Kroni was the right-hand demon to the ruler of the underworld. He was powerful, dangerous, and had a terrible temper.

"And he's in the blackened flesh he enjoys so much." Frank snorted. "I do not see the appeal. Too theatrical for my taste. Typical Kroni."

"Axel's father is a soul collector."

"Correct."

I swallowed my fear. Not many demons made my knees shake, but soul collectors were the stuff of nightmares. They used to be all about collecting damned souls and tossing them into fiery pits. But they'd diversified and now used their powers so anyone could bargain with them. If you had a pure soul, you could sell it to a soul collector and get your hands on a lot of power. Soul collectors didn't care who they did business with, so long as the price was right.

Another angel was downed along with a gang member as I stared open-mouthed at the fight.

Wiggles raced over. "This is great. People would pay money to see a fight like this."

I shook myself to dislodge some of the horror I felt. "Maybe they would, but it's time for it to stop."

"I don't recommend you go up against Kroni," Frank whispered in my head. "He's not known for his benevolent behavior. He does not like witches."

I watched Kroni slam dunk an angel like she was a basketball. "I don't love the angels, and the gang is a massive pain in my backside, but I can't watch them die."

"You could," Frank said. "It will be entertaining. Your hellhound has the right idea."

"Tempest, we should sit this one out," Wiggles said. "You've got magic skills, but this is a huge, raging mad demon who wants to kill everyone in sight."

"He's also Axel's father," I said.

"Huh! No way! Axel is nothing like him. This dude is seriously cool." Wiggles studied Kroni. "Nope, that is not Axel's dad."

"Fortunately for us, he is." I inched closer as Kroni hurled an enormous fireball at the remaining gang members, and they scattered.

I sucked in a breath. There was never a good time to approach a demon, but I handled demons almost every day. This one would be no different. Hopefully, maybe. Oh, bugger, what was I getting myself into?

I rolled my shoulders and walked toward Kroni. "You don't need to attack. I summoned you."

Kroni spun on his heel and stalked toward me. I backed up several steps and held my hands up. There were rules for handling angry demons. Rule number one: Don't rile them any more than necessary. Rule number two: They do not enjoy being summoned. Rule number three: If you summon a demon, you'd better have an excellent reason for trying to control them. Rule number four: If you don't have a good reason, you need to have your affairs in order, because they will destroy you.

The air around me felt hot and murky as Kroni drew close. "I did not mean to cause offense, but your son was in mortal danger."

Kroni raised his chin and sniffed the air, his huge nostrils contracting and expanding several times. "A Crypt witch." His voice was low and gravelly like he smoked unfiltered cigarettes.

"Tempest Crypt. I'm friends with Axel."

His top lip curled, revealing a fine set of sharp teeth. "My son is friends with a witch. How disappointing."

"It's not so hard to believe. Everyone in Willow Tree Falls gets along."

Kroni grunted. A flame shot out of his mouth and hit the ground. "Who placed my son in danger?"

"I'm not certain. We have someone cursing people and burying them alive. I didn't have enough time to save Axel and the other cursed victim, so I decided to get assistance from you."

"There is more than one victim?"

"There would have been four. I saved one guy, and you saved Axel. The others weren't so lucky."

Kroni shook his head. "You lie. You did not summon me."

I shrugged. "Technically, it wasn't me. Does that matter?"

Kroni's muscled arm shot out so fast I didn't see him move. His talons wrapped around my neck, and he squeezed. I wished I had my demon catching bag. I did not want to try to swallow this big guy. He would give me a nasty case of acid reflux and most likely make me explode from the inside.

He sniffed the air again. "I thought so. You are the witch who houses a demon inside her."

"You've heard of me?" I gasped as his talons scraped my skin.

"Most demons have." He snarled in my face. "You are an aberration."

"We all have to make a living."

"Dad, don't hurt her." Axel was on his knees, staring at us, his eyes wide and his face pale and mud-streaked.

Kroni did not turn. "She means something to you?"

"Tempest is telling the truth. We are friends."

Kroni's gaze ran over me. "My son is an idiot."

"He has his moments," I said.

"Please, don't kill her." Axel staggered to his feet, made it two steps, and fell on his face. My hero.

Kroni belched sulfur over me. "He seems fond of you. I shall spare your life."

Dazielle made the hideous mistake of jumping on Kroni's back as he dropped me to the ground.

He roared, spouting fire from his mouth as he reached around and flung her over his shoulder.

I shook my head and groaned as I watched her collapse to the ground. Just when I was getting somewhere, the angels had to mess things up.

As more angels charged Kroni, I ducked behind him and knelt next to Axel, turning him gently onto his back. "How are you doing?"

"I think I died a couple of times." Axel's eyes rolled back in his head.

I tapped his cheek. "Stay with me. It was a close call, but you're breathing now."

Axel coughed and spat mud on the ground. "I can't believe you summoned my father. I didn't even know you could do that."

"It was Frank. They're old acquaintances. It was the only way I could save you and Rhett at the same time."

"Rhett was cursed too?" Axel forced his eyes open.

"He was. Did you see who cursed you? I don't think they're going to stop, so we have to stop them."

A shriek echoed through the forest, followed by another explosion, as Kroni launched himself at the remaining gang members who had crept back after his last attack.

We both cringed as the fight grew nearer and a blast of fire skimmed the ground by my feet.

Axel feebly brushed at a burning bush next to us before giving up and flopping to the ground. "I remember some of what happened."

"You saw who cursed you?"

Axel ran a hand down his face, smearing sticky mud across his cheeks. "The memory is hazy. I don't remember anything after being cursed, other than feeling sick and a little terrified. I definitely don't remember coming here."

I grabbed his shoulders. "Axel, think really carefully. Other peoples' lives depend on this. Who cursed you?"

Axel's gaze widened as he stared at me. "Oh, no! Tempest, you're not safe. You have to stay away from Cloven Hoof."

I frowned. That was the exact same thing Rhett had said. "Is it one of my bar staff? Is it Izzie?"

An angel was thrown through the air and slammed into Axel, sending them both flying into a tree.

I jumped up and hurried over. I yanked the unconscious angel off Axel, but I was too late to get an answer to my question. He was out cold.

"No! That was my chance to find out who cursed Axel." I glared at Kroni.

"My son is injured, again?" The demon strode over and scooped Axel up with one hand, peering into his slack face and giving him a shake.

I looked behind Kroni and saw the carnage he'd left. Trees were burnt, angels were down, and there were no signs of any gang members, other than a crumpled, blood-stained leather jacket.

I returned my attention to Kroni. "What do you expect? You threw an angel at him. Those things are heavy."

"It's the wings. Axel is simply a casualty of war." Kroni sniffed Axel. "He won't die."

"This isn't a war. If you'd bothered to talk to the angels or the gang members, they'd have told you what was happening."

"Angels never listen to demons. When I arrived, I had to assume the angels and the leather-clad cretins were trying to kill Axel." He lifted Axel closer and tucked him under an arm. "I will take him with me."

"Stop him," Dazielle croaked from her position on the ground.

"You have got to be kidding," I muttered. "He came to help."

"He's a wanted demon," Dazielle said. "Tempest, do your job."

My gaze ran over Kroni. Here was a problem. Technically, when I see a demon who's doing bad things, I bag the demon and stop him, but Kroni was helping Axel.

"The angels have you on a hit list," I said.

A slow smile spread across Kroni's face. "What number am I?"

I arched an eyebrow. "I have no idea."

"He's number three," Dazielle muttered.

"Be quiet, angel." Kroni blasted a flame at her, and she covered her head with a wing.

I took a step toward Dazielle, but her wings were flame retardant, and the fire faded quickly.

"Hmph. That is disappointing news. I must try harder." Kroni used a talon to scratch the end of his nose.

I turned to Kroni. "At what?"

"Becoming number one on the angels' hit list." Kroni's smile widened. "When I achieve that lofty goal, shall I expect a visit from you, witch? Will you gobble me up like that devil hiding inside you?"

I did not fancy my chances against Axel's dad. He was a mean son of a demon. "If you're lucky."

Kroni raised his head and chuckled. "Then until we meet."

"Perhaps when you next visit Axel in Willow Tree Falls. You can always come in quietly if you're bored of life as a fugitive. I can get you a nice place in our prison."

"I doubt I will return." Kroni sniffed the air and scowled. "I do not like the neighborhood. It has not been welcoming during my short visit."

"It could have something to do with you blowing up the place."

Kroni looked around. "I have done worse."

I looked at Axel, who was still unconscious. "I hope he'll be okay."

"He will recover. I will make sure of it. Axel is not as strong as me, but even a half-demon recovers much faster than mere mortals. You will have Axel back if he desires to return." Kroni stamped on the ground. A flash of flame flared and engulfed him and Axel.

As I blinked the image off my retinas and wafted away the sulfur stench, I saw they had gone.

Wiggles trotted over, his tongue hanging out and his tail up. "That was epic. I've never seen such an incredible fight. Axel's dad is awesome. How come Axel is such a jerk when he has such a cool father?

Hey, I wonder if I can do that stamping on the ground and vanishing trick. Hellhounds and demons aren't so different." Wiggles bounded around, stamping his stubby legs on the ground and trying to make flames appear.

"You'll have to ask Kroni how he does that trick." I walked to the first downed angel, who was just coming round. One of her wings was bent at an unnatural angle, and she had blood on her face.

"We'd better get more help out here." I checked on another angel. "Wiggles, go to the hospital and get some medics."

Wiggles looked around. "Everyone looks okay to me. It's just a bit of blood and a few torn feathers."

"Get out of here, you lazy hound. They need our help."

He grumbled for a few seconds before running off.

I knelt next to Dazielle and lifted the wing that covered her face.

She blinked up at me. "You let him go?"

"The big, bad demon has gone, and he's taken his son with him."

She stared at me. "His son?"

"Yes, that was Axel's father. Didn't you know Kroni was his dad?"

"I don't spend any time with Axel." Dazielle let out a sigh. "I knew he had a demon father, but that was it."

"Kroni was protecting his son from what he thought was a joint attack by angels and bikers."

"How did he know Axel was in danger?" Dazielle tried to sit up but only succeeded in moving an inch before slumping back and lying in a cloud of white feathers that drifted around us.

I cleared my throat. "Don't get mad, but Frank summoned him."

"Tempest!" Dazielle said weakly. "We do not summon demons to Willow Tree Falls."

"If there had been any other choice, I'd have done it," I said. "It was a case of saving either Rhett or Axel. Frank discovered where they'd been buried, but there wasn't time to uncover them both. You were fighting with the gang rather than doing your job, so I had to do it. I make no apologies for wanting to keep my friends alive."

Dazielle finally managed to get up onto her elbows and looked around. "He's destroyed my angels."

"They'll recover. They're hardy."

Jimmy Blackmouth emerged through the trees, limping heavily. Supported on his arm was Rhett.

I jumped up and hurried over. "You found him!"

"Your hellhound told me where he was," Jimmy said. "I slipped away from the fight to make sure he was okay."

As I got closer, I realized Rhett was unconscious. "Did he say anything when you found him?"

"Only a few dozen curse words. The effort of getting up off the ground knocked him out again."

I sighed. It looks like the curse had really messed with Rhett.

Dazielle hobbled over slowly, wincing with every step. "That curse will have exhausted him. The best thing is rest and some magic juice at the hospital. We'll arrange to have him taken there."

"Rhett hates hospitals," Jimmy said.

"He's unconscious, so he doesn't get a say in what happens to him," I said. "I've got medics coming. They'll be here soon."

"Good," Dazielle said. "I'll need statements from everyone. This will take a while to process."

"You can have my statement later." I needed to get to Cloven Hoof and confront Izzie. I glanced at Dazielle. Should I tell the angels about my suspicions? Axel had been taken by Kroni, and Rhett was unconscious, so they couldn't reveal who the curse killer was.

If Izzie was involved, I needed to know why she'd done it. What had Serath, Dewey, Rhett, and Axel done to her that meant she'd cursed them and buried them alive as punishment?

"When Wiggles gets back with the medics, tell him to meet me at Cloven Hoof."

"You're leaving?" Dazielle looked alarmed. "You're one of the few people left standing."

"You've got a handle on this, and the medics won't be long."

Dazielle sighed. "I want you at the station first thing tomorrow. Full statement, no compromise."

I took a step away. I had to get to Izzie. "Sure, whatever you need."

Dazielle glared at me. "What are you up to?"

"Nothing. You've got everything in hand. Rhett and Axel are safe, and the demon has gone. You don't need me here. I'll only get in your way."

"What about the curse killer?" Dazielle asked. "We still don't know who it is. She's still out there."

"We'll have to catch her tomorrow," I said. "You can get information out of Rhett when he wakes up."

Dazielle lifted Rhett's head and dropped it back so it flopped against Jimmy's shoulder. "I doubt he'll be awake for some time. What about Axel? When is his father bringing him back?"

I continued to creep away. "He didn't say."

"Which means we're no closer to finding our curse killer." Dazielle watched me with narrowed eyes.

I bit my tongue. I didn't want the angels involved, not yet. Not until I knew the truth and the reasons Izzie had done this.

"Get out of here," Dazielle said with a sigh. "But I want to speak to you soon. We've got a killer to find."

We! When did I become an official member of Angel Force? Still, I had no time to argue with Dazielle over that. "You know where I am." I turned on my heel and ran through the forest.

It was time to confront Izzie and find out how she was involved in this mess.

Chapter 19

The sun was dipping below the horizon as I reached Cloven Hoof. I pulled open the door and hurried through.

Merrie looked up from behind the bar, and her mouth fell open. "Tempest! What have you been doing?"

"Where's Izzie?"

"She's out back, unloading a delivery," Merrie said. "Is something wrong?"

"You could say that. I just helped the angels save Rhett and Axel. The curse killer got them. We almost lost them."

"That's terrible," Merrie said. "But wait, what has Izzie got to do with this? You can't still think she's involved."

"That's what I need to ask her." I hurried to the storage room at the back of the bar and found Izzie unloading boxes from a cart.

Her smile faded when she looked at me. "Gosh, Tempest. You look like you've been mud wrestling."

"Leave that." I caught hold of her arm and pulled her away. I didn't want to do this. Everything in my gut told me this was wrong. I knew Izzie. She was fun and clever and great with the customers. What had gone so badly wrong that she'd curse Rhett and Axel and kill the others?

"What's the matter?" Concern filtered across Izzie's face. "Did a customer make a complaint about me?"

"Our customers love you. It's not that. What happened between you, Axel, and Rhett?"

"I know they're missing," Izzie said slowly. "People have been looking for them. Is that what this is about?"

"When did you last see them?"

Izzie chewed on her bottom lip. "I saw Axel in Cloven Hoof about five days ago. You were chatting to him. As for Rhett, I'm not sure. We don't mingle in the same circles. What are you getting at?"

"Have either of them done anything to annoy you?"

"No! Axel is a bit of a flirt, which can be distracting when we're busy. I don't know Rhett all that well. If we do speak, he usually asks after you."

"Did you recently visit either of them in their homes?"

"Never! I don't understand why you're asking me these questions."

I let out a sigh. Honestly, neither did I. It couldn't be Izzie. She couldn't be the curse killer. "Rhett and

Axel were taken by the curse killer."

Izzie's hand flew to her mouth. "I had no idea. Are they okay?"

I narrowed my eyes. She seemed genuinely surprised. "We got them out in time."

Izzie let out a sigh. "That's a relief. The poor guys. Why were they targeted?"

"I was hoping it was a question you could answer," I said.

"Me! I have nothing to do with this."

I rubbed my forehead with my fingers. "I don't want to believe you're involved. You're great at your job. I consider you a friend."

"But? What aren't you saying?"

"You did date Serath, and I saw you when he came to Cloven Hoof that first night. He said something to offend you. I'd never seen you react that way with a customer."

Izzie's eyes narrowed. "You're right. He was rude to me. I was shocked to see Serath and reacted badly. He made some smug comment about his friends having me because he'd already sampled the goods and didn't want to go there again."

I scowled and shook my head. "That's disgusting."

"It was. And, to be clear, I never got that friendly with Serath. We had a kiss and a cuddle but nothing else. He was so crude. The only way I could stop myself from slapping him was to take a step back. I was relieved when Merrie came to my rescue. I didn't want to cause a scene, but Serath was an idiot. That doesn't mean I wanted him dead. And I have no problems with the others. I like Rhett and Axel."

"Can you do curse magic?"

Izzie glanced away. "If I want to, which I don't. The worst magic I used on Serath was that belching spell, and I've already told you about that. It was a little revenge. That's all I did to him."

I really wanted to believe Izzie. I wanted her to be innocent.

"Tempest, you must believe me. I'm not the curse killer. I wouldn't do that. I love being in Willow Tree Falls. I have friends here, and this place is great. You can't think it's me."

I tipped my head back and looked at the ceiling. Maybe the warnings Rhett and Axel had given me were about something else or someone else.

"Who else can do curse magic here?"

Izzie scratched her head. "Well, apart from me, Merrie, I expect. Paula, not a chance, nor Niall. I don't know Ginger and Blaze that well, but they don't seem like strong magic users. I've seen Blaze do fire magic, but nothing stronger than that."

"Is everyone here tonight?"

"No, Paula is off." Izzie stared at me. "You don't think someone here is the curse killer, do you?"

The door to the storage room banged open. Merrie, Blaze, and Ginger walked through. They pulled up short when they saw me holding onto Izzie.

Izzie gripped my hand. "Tempest, I don't know how I'm going to convince you that I'm innocent.

These curses have nothing to do with me. You have to believe me."

"I do." I sighed and loosened my grip on Izzie. "But Rhett and Axel said Cloven Hoof isn't safe."

"What are you talking about?" Merrie walked over with the others. "Cloven Hoof is a safe place. We keep it safe."

"I don't think it is, not anymore. Rhett and Axel said it's not safe. It's because somebody here is the curse killer."

Merrie gasped and shook her head.

Ginger's cheeks paled, and she took a step back. Her hand reached for Blaze, who looked equally as shocked.

Blaze shook his head. "None of us are involved. We were working when the killings happened."

"That's not proof enough of innocence. The curse isn't the thing that kills. It immobilizes its victims. Whoever placed the curse on these guys buries them in a shallow grave. They suffocate to death. The curse holds them in place while they die."

"That's a terrible thing to do," Merrie said. "None of us would do that."

Ginger inched backwards toward the door, dropping her hold on Blaze, her hands clenched. "I'm not feeling so good. It's too gross thinking about what's going on."

"Ginger, wait! I'm not finished. I have to know for sure why Cloven Hoof isn't a safe place." I stared at her hard. I didn't know much about Ginger, but that didn't mean I didn't trust her. She had a great resume, loads of experience, and she'd been nothing but brilliant with the customers. I had no reason to believe she was involved any more than I did Izzie or Blaze.

"I've already told you I'm not involved. I feel faint. I need air." She turned on her heel and raced out the door.

I exchanged a surprised glance with Merrie. "Is she running because she's guilty?"

"Ginger wouldn't waste her magic on cursing people she barely knows." Merrie stared at the swinging door Ginger had run through.

"You don't run unless you have something to hide." I raced into the bar. There was no sign of Ginger, but the bathroom door was swinging shut.

I hurried over and peered inside. "Ginger, what do you know?" I inched inside. She wasn't by the basins.

I checked the first three toilet cubicles. All empty. "If you're involved, it's better if you come clean. Rhett and Axel are safe. They've seen their attacker. If it was you, the angels will know soon enough."

The next door swung open. A stranger stared back at me, her dark eyes wide with surprise. "Oh! How did you get in here?"

The woman blinked. "I just needed to use the bathroom. Am I in trouble?"

I studied her before looking away, realizing I was staring at a woman sitting on the loo. "Sure. Have you seen a redhead come in here?"

"No, I've only been here a minute. I didn't hear anyone else come in."

I glanced back at her. She wasn't a stranger, but I couldn't place her face. That long, dark hair and those dark brown eyes were familiar. "Do I know you?"

She tugged at the door. "No. If you don't mind, I'm right in the middle of something."

I let the door swing shut but remained outside. I knew that face.

"You're still there," the woman said. "I can hear you breathing."

"I'm going." I walked to the door leading back to the club and pretended to leave, holding my breath as I did so.

After a minute, the toilet door opened. The woman poked her head out. As our gazes locked, I gasped. Her eyes were black, and dark magic oozed from her like sticky treacle.

She grimaced and shook her head as she emerged from the toilet. "I knew you wouldn't leave this alone."

"I know you."

"We've already established that's not true."

"No, I do." I recalled the clippings I found in Serath's bag. "You're Sandy Bishop!"

She tilted her head. "So what if I am?"

I shook my head. My vision was playing tricks on me. One second, I saw Ginger and the next Sandy. But Sandy had been missing for five years. How was she suddenly in the bathroom of Cloven Hoof?

Sandy stepped closer, her fists clenched. "Mind if I leave?"

Before I could answer, she blasted me with a knockback spell and fled out the door.

My stomach throbbed from the sudden attack, but I hurried after her.

I skidded to a halt in the bar. Sandy was smashing bottles of whiskey on the floor.

She ignited a fireball in the palm of her hand when she saw me. "You come any closer and this whole place goes up."

"Why are you doing this?" I stayed where I was, not wanting to see my beautiful bar go up in flames. "Do you have something to do with what happened to the dead guys? Did you put those curses on them?"

"You won't understand. You've always had it so easy. It's not that easy for everybody. I had to protect myself."

I risked taking a step closer. "What are you talking about? Did Serath do something bad to you?"

"I warn you. Stop moving or your precious Cloven Hoof is gone."

"I'm staying right here. Why don't you tell me why you're here?" I rubbed my eyes, not believing what I saw. One second, Ginger stood there; the next it was Sandy. The constant flow of dark magic from this woman made me dizzy.

Sandy sneered at me. "Am I making you feel bad?"

I nodded and staggered to the side.

She lowered the fireball and waved her hands from the top of her head down her body. As she did so, her features stopped shifting, and the surrounding air crackled.

I blinked and took a step back. Ginger was gone.

Chapter 20

I turned as I heard a door open and gestured Merrie, Blaze, and Izzie back as they appeared from out of the store room.

Ginger, now revealed to be Sandy, glared at them and raised her palm. Fire flared around her in a protective circle.

"Who's that?" Merrie asked, her eyes wide.

I sucked in a breath. "Sandy Bishop."

"I'm surprised you remember me." Sandy's gaze remained on me.

"I remember you. You've been missing for years. Everyone wondered what had happened to you."

"Hold on, Sandy Bishop?" Merrie stared at her. "You used to live on the edge of the forest."

"That's right," Sandy said. "I lived with my mom. I was happy, content living a simple life. I never wanted any trouble. But trouble found me."

"What trouble found you?" I asked. "What made you leave Willow Tree Falls all those years ago?"

"I never left," Sandy hissed. "I've been here the whole time."

The entrance door to Cloven Hoof slammed open. Dazielle barged through with Wiggles racing along behind her.

He bounced over to me. "I tried to out-run the angel, but she's fast. She knows you're up to something. Who's this?" Wiggles looked at Sandy.

"I think it's our curse killer," I said.

"You can't prove that." Sandy lunged at Dazielle, flinging the fireball she held at her head.

Dazielle barely fluttered out of the way in time, obviously still suffering from her injuries. She landed flat on her back, and Sandy jumped on top of her.

I raced over and wrapped an arm around Sandy, hauling her off Dazielle. Sandy's viscose, foul magic crept across my arm, and I quickly let her go.

Sandy turned and glowered at me. "Friends with the angels now, witch."

Dazielle scrambled to her feet, her expression wary. "You said this is the curse killer? I've never seen her before."

"None of us have seen her for five years," I said. "This is Sandy Bishop. She went missing."

Dazielle blinked slowly, recognition filling her eyes. "We thought you'd left the village."

Sandy shook her head, her dark hair sticking to her forehead. "I didn't leave. I was taken against my will."

REVENGE OF THE WITCH

"By whom?" I asked.

Sandy cracked her neck from side to side and flexed her fingers. She was preparing for another battle. "I'd only been free for a couple of days when I heard Puddles Lavern bragging about Dewey and his friends coming for a visit."

"Free from where?" I asked.

Sandy continued as if she hadn't heard me. "I was a mess after so long in confinement, struggling to understand what had happened to me. When I heard Puddles, it all came back. And when I heard her say Serath's name, I remembered everything he'd done."

"What's Serath got to do with you going missing?" Dazielle asked.

My breath caught in my throat. "Serath took you five years ago. What did he do?"

"He cursed me," Sandy said. "He was angry because I turned him down. He tried a pathetic seduction spell on me. It failed, and I wasn't interested in him. He showed up at my house one evening, being sweet and charming, but there was something off with him. Serath tried another spell, but it didn't work. I called him out on it, and he walked off in a huff. I thought that was the end of it."

"Serath decided to get revenge," I said.

Sandy bared her teeth as she nodded. "He was better at magic than I realized. I was taking a walk the next night, and he found me. I tried to be polite, but he wouldn't take no for an answer. He grabbed me, and that's the last clear memory I have. I woke up a few times, but I couldn't move. He used a curse on me. I was terrified. I thought he was going to kill me."

"Then what happened?"

Black sparks flew off Sandy as she shuddered. "He did what I did to him. While I was still cursed and couldn't move, he buried me alive as a punishment for turning him down. He said if he couldn't have me, no man would."

"How did you survive?" Horror filled Dazielle's eyes.

"I almost didn't. Serath came back to Willow Tree Falls every six months to check on me and strengthen his magic. I knew when it was getting close to his visit because the curse would weaken, and I'd be able to move. On one occasion, I almost dug my way out. I had my hand free and could breathe clean air. Serath caught me, laughed in my face, and reburied me. He told me it was no less than I deserved."

"You were buried for five years?" I couldn't hide how disgusted I was. Serath was a monster.

"He left me underground with a small tube, so I could breathe. Every time he came back, he would perform magic to ensure I didn't starve or die of dehydration. There were times when it came close, though. As I said, his magic wasn't perfect. And the breathing tube he left me got blocked several times. I've lost count of the number of times I fell unconscious because I had so little air to breathe."

"How did you finally get out?" Dazielle asked.

"Serath's magic failed. I don't know what happened. He must have been late in coming to revitalize the magic. That was my chance to get out, so I took it."

"That's right," I said. "I remember Puddles being upset about Dewey and his friends changing their plans at the last minute."

"That would be it," Sandy said. "That arrogant jerk believed his magic would hold for longer than it did. It was enough for me to break the curse and get out of that hole. It felt incredible to be able to move and breathe freely. But I was weak and confused for days."

"How did you get to be in Cloven Hoof?" Dazielle asked. "Why disguise yourself as Ginger?"

"I hadn't planned to. My first thought was to get to my mom. I needed to let her know I was okay. I was stumbling out of the forest when I heard Puddles. She was talking about the upcoming visit with Dewey, Serath, and Bart. That's when I knew I'd been given a chance to get revenge. After everything Serath put me through, he had to pay. That became my priority. I had a few weeks to recover, so I headed back into the forest, only coming out at night."

"To do what?"

"Get strong. I even broke into the hospital and got magic to speed up my recovery. After that, all I did was practice the curse. I had to get it right. Serath could not be allowed to get away with this."

"You disguised yourself as Ginger because you knew Serath would turn up at Cloven Hoof?" I recalled the day Ginger had walked in almost a month ago. She'd been so sure of herself. She knew her way around the bar and had poured the perfect pint. I'd had no clue what she was hiding. She was a strong witch. A better witch than me.

Sandy nodded. "I knew Serath wouldn't be able to resist this place. That night, when he came in with the others, I was so shocked I almost couldn't move. I didn't want to draw attention to myself, even with my disguise in place."

"He noticed you when he was talking to me and said you seemed familiar." Izzie stood by the storeroom door with the others.

"I couldn't risk getting too close to Serath in case he saw through my magic. I had to act fast. I had to curse him and bury him before he figured out what had happened. He wouldn't have waited long before going into the forest and strengthening his curse. If he'd gone to the site I was buried in and discovered me gone, he'd have known something was wrong. He'd have fled Willow Tree Falls, knowing I'd have been after him."

I looked at Dazielle. "I don't blame Ginger, or rather Sandy, for what she's done. I'd have done the same thing if some scumbag cursed me and shoved me in the ground because I turned him down for a date."

Dazielle simply arched an eyebrow. "What about the others? Why curse Dewey?"

"Dewey got suspicious. I overheard him and Serath talking about me. Serath was convinced he knew me, and Dewey was staring when they were at the bar, trying to figure out where they knew me from. I'm

REVENGE OF THE WITCH

not the best at disguise magic, and if I'd let it slip for a second, it might have ruined everything. When I get tired or nervous, the magic wavers. I had to get rid of Dewey in case he blew my cover."

"That doesn't explain what you did to Rhett and Axel," Dazielle said.

"Rhett spends a lot of time in the forest," I said to Sandy. "Did he see what you were doing and try to stop you?"

"He got unlucky," Sandy said. "I didn't mean to curse him, but he walked right into my path as I was placing Dewey in the ground. I tried to explain it away and said it was nothing, but he wouldn't let it go. Rhett insisted he look at what I was burying. I couldn't let him see, so I flung the curse at him, and he collapsed."

"You were going to kill Rhett to hide your secret?" I shook my head. I could let her off for Serath but not Rhett.

Sandy scowled at me. "He probably deserved it. I bet Rhett hasn't treated women kindly. He lets them down and breaks their hearts. Most men do. When they don't get what they want, they turn mean."

"So, Rhett was unfortunate, but what about Axel?" Dazielle asked.

Sandy snorted a laugh. "I've seen Axel in action. Whenever he's in here, he flirts with everyone. He got on the wrong side of me one night. He'd had too much to drink and kept pestering me for mushrooms. He offered all sorts of incentives, but then suggested we go back to his place and have some private fun. I put him in his place, but he wouldn't stop. It brought back the memories of how Serath had treated me the night he took me, cursed me, and threw me in the ground. All because I didn't want him."

Axel did tend to flirt too hard, but cursing him for doing it was extreme.

"You went to Axel's with mushrooms because you knew he wouldn't be able to resist them." I recalled seeing the bag of mushrooms in his house.

"He's not safe to be around," Sandy said. "He pushed too hard. It was only right I pushed back. I grabbed a bag of mushrooms at the end of my last shift and headed to his place in the morning. He was happy to let me in. He practically drooled over the mushrooms. He made us both coffee, and I chatted and pretended to flirt to get him to relax."

"Then you cursed him," I said. "You took him to the woods and buried him."

"I used a cloaking spell and dragged him into the swamp. I'd have left him like the others, but I heard the angels fighting. I adjusted the curse speed to finish Axel off quickly. I wanted him to suffer and slowly suffocate, but I had to change my plans."

"I understand why you wanted revenge on Serath," I said. "But you can't attack and curse innocent people."

"You know Rhett better than everyone else," Sandy sneered. "He's not innocent. And as for Axel, I've seen you having to fend him off. You can't say they didn't have it coming."

"They didn't deserve that. Give them a slap and tell them to keep their hands off but don't curse them and bury them alive."

"I thought you'd be on my side," Sandy said. "We got on well when I was Ginger."

"I was friends with Ginger Gibson. It turns out she's not real." I felt sad that I'd lost Ginger. It was horribly unfair what had happened to Sandy, but she couldn't get away with this.

"You need to come with me," Dazielle said. "I need your full confession before you are charged."

More black sparks flew from Sandy, and she hunched over and growled. "I'm not going to prison. I was defending myself. I was righting a wrong."

"Two people are dead because of you," I said. "Admittedly, they were jerks, but you have to pay for what you've done."

Sandy flung her arms out, and flames shot toward the ceiling.

I looked over at Merrie, Izzie, and Blaze. "Get out of here!"

"We can't leave you," Merrie said.

"Get in the back. That's an order." If I was worried about protecting them, I wouldn't be able to focus on bringing down Sandy.

"We're staying." Merrie jammed her hands on her hips.

"If you all want to keep your jobs, you leave. Now!" I hated pulling rank, but it was for their own good.

Merrie frowned at me before ushering Izzie and Blaze away.

I'd make my apologies later, but I could only do that if they were all alive.

Dazielle fluffed out her wings. I could see one wasn't working properly and hung at her side. She was in no shape to fight Sandy.

I hurried to her side. "You stay out of this. I'll deal with Sandy. After all, I made the mistake of hiring her."

Dazielle shook her head. "Be careful, Tempest. She's got serious magic going on inside her."

"Yes, and it's singeing my bar. This has to stop." I raised my hands and flung a dousing spell at her fire to stop the flames.

Sandy raised a magical barrier, and my magic bounced off.

We threw several more spells at each other. She favored fire, and I just favored staying alive and not turning crispy. I felt the painful sting of dark magic kiss my skin as her power got too close.

"She's working up to something big." Wiggles bounced on his paws as he stood on top of a table, watching the fight.

"She's already doing something big." I dodged a spell. "I can't hold her for much longer."

"Maybe Frank can," Wiggles said.

I felt around for Frank's energy, but he was nowhere to be found. "He's content to sit this one out. He must figure I can handle things on my own."

"Maybe you'd like to be cursed yourself." Sandy splayed her fingers, and a jet of what looked like a black spider web shot toward me.

"Look out! It's her curse." Wiggles launched himself off the table and knocked me sideways. The curse missed me by an inch but slammed into Dazielle, who was flung backward into the wall.

"Thanks, that was close," I said to Wiggles as I clambered to my feet.

Wiggles looked at Dazielle, who was pinned to the wall, her arms and legs flailing and one wing flapping. "That angel wouldn't have been any help, anyway."

A fireball slammed by my feet. I swung and kept flinging spells at Sandy. Her focus was not on me as she concentrated on pinning Dazielle to the wall as the curse spread from her feet, up her legs, and across her torso, winding black strands of power across her.

Dazielle continued to struggle, but in her injured state, she couldn't break free from Sandy's magic.

"No more spells. This needs direct action." I flung myself at Sandy and wrapped my arms around her.

We fell to the floor, and she twisted in my grip before grabbing hold of me. Her curse was still active, and it pulsed across my skin.

"You won't stop me," Sandy spat in my face. "I will have my revenge."

"No, you don't." I flared my own power, and our energies smashed together. My magic was not at full strength, having drained it healing Rhett. I hoped I had enough in the tank to take this crazed witch down.

I felt straightaway that she was stronger. Sandy wasn't a demon, so my magic was less effective against her, but she was something dark and deadly and couldn't be allowed to leave this bar.

"My witch magic trumps you, demon slayer," she hissed.

Her curse was too strong for me, and I felt my limbs grow weak as she siphoned my ability to move.

Sandy struggled out from underneath me and rolled to her knees. "Now you're going to pay. You—"

A roar reverberated around the room, and a blast of flame slammed into Sandy's back. She shrieked and rolled away.

I turned to see Wiggles belching fire. My jaw dropped open. "I didn't know you could do that."

He looked as confused as I did. "Neither did I. Who knew, in times of crisis, I belch fire?"

The door to the bar flew open. Three angels zoomed through, their wings spreading out as they took in the carnage in front of them.

"Get her," Wiggles yelled and pointed his nose at Sandy.

The angels turned to Dazielle for confirmation, but she could only nod. The power of speech had already left her as the curse took hold.

They descended on Sandy, who bucked and twisted and threw fire and sticky dark webs of curse at them.

One angel was thrown away and slammed to the ground in a heap of feathers.

Sandy screamed as she was covered by the remaining angels, and after a struggle that had the room stinking of burning feathers and sour magic, they got her under control.

Wiggles nudged me with his nose. "Having fun?"

"I can't move. Sandy got me with her curse." I rolled pathetically from side to side.

He shoved my arm with a paw. "Who's going to feed me if you can't move?"

I scowled at him. "I'm trapped in a curse and all you care about is your stomach."

"If you don't have fuel in your belly, you can't function." Wiggles turned to the angels. "We need some help over here."

An angel hurried over. "What happened?" It was Cassiel, her face smeared with soot and sweat dappling her normally perfect brow. She offered me her hand.

"You've just arrested the curse killer," I said. "I can't move, and I might not be able to speak soon. Sandy cursed me and Dazielle with the same magic she used on Serath, Dewey, and the others."

Cassiel's eyes widened. She looked dazed as if not knowing what to do next. There was no one in charge to give her any orders.

I tilted my head. "Maybe you can start by helping your boss."

"Oh! Yes, good idea. Thanks, Tempest." Cassiel hurried over to where Dazielle was slowly sliding down the wall.

Wiggles placed his paws on my chest. "That was quite an adventure. Same time next week?"

I could barely move my head as the dark magic spread through me. "Maybe not. We deserve a couple of weeks off after this."

"We caught the curse killer," Wiggles said. "We have to celebrate."

"When I can move again, we will." My throat felt tight as the curse edged across me.

Wiggles licked my cheek. "Don't worry. I'll keep an eye on you until you shake this off."

"Thanks, Wiggles. You saved my life."

"And got Dazielle blasted with a curse. It was so worth it."

I felt a little tearful as my best buddy rested on my chest and chatted about the epic fight he'd seen.

"You're a great hellhound," I whispered.

"That's what I'm here for. Saving lives, breaking hearts, and generally being awesome." He belched sulfur in my face. I could do nothing but inhale it and accept Wiggles, sulfurous gas and all.

"I'll get you a big treat." Those were the last words I spoke as the curse took away my ability to speak.

"I'll make a list." Wiggles looked at me. "But before you do that, isn't there someone you need to check on?"

I wrinkled my brow. It was the most movement he'd get out of me for a while.

"A certain hot guy who's life you saved and who will want to thank you by giving you a nice, wet, slobbery kiss?"

I shut my eyes and pretended to sleep. That was a problem I had no clue how to handle. I'd saved Rhett first and picked him over Axel, but did that mean anything significant, and if so, what would happen next?

Chapter 21

It had been two days since Sandy's arrest. She was safely tucked away where no one would find her. And, after twelve hours of not being able to move or speak, her curse had finally broken, and I was back to normal.

"I can't believe that lovely young Ginger was a black-hearted villain," Granny Dottie said.

The whole family, apart from Aurora, who was on cemetery duty, sat around the table in Mom's kitchen.

"She had us all fooled," I said. "Ginger Gibson was an awesome person. Sandy Bishop, not so much."

"That poor child must have been half-mad to do what she did." Mom placed a sweet-smelling stack of pancakes on the table. "That dreadful boy treated her appallingly just because she rejected him and his ego couldn't take it."

"I hope the angels go easy on her," Auntie Queenie said.

"I've talked to Dazielle. She sees the mitigating circumstances but will still charge Sandy with the attempted murder of Rhett and Axel. Sandy also killed Dewey to cover her tracks. She might be crazy, but she's not stupid."

"Which means the poor dear will not be back in Willow Tree Falls anytime soon," Mom said. "Tempest, you should go visit her."

"Mom! She cursed me."

"Well, I will visit her. And her mom needs to know what happened."

"She's been informed," I said. "She was as shocked as everybody. Happy to know her daughter is alive but horrified by what she'd done."

"With Sandy gone, does that mean you're looking for a new member of staff?" Granny Dottie asked. "I can take a few shifts in the bar if you're short staffed."

"You, behind my bar." I shook my head. Granny Dottie had a liking for hard liquor. "We'll manage fine for now. Although, this proves I'm not a great judge of character. I don't think I'll do any new hires for a while. I didn't spot the dark magic on Sandy."

"Nonsense," Mom said. "You weren't looking for any dark magic. Why would you? All your other bar staff are lovely. And that Blaze is a proper hunk. I saw him the other day with his shirt off."

"Where did you see him with no shirt on?" I asked.

Mom blushed. "He didn't have his blinds down in his bedroom. I was just walking past and glanced up."

"Mom! You're a peeping tom."

"No, I'm not! It's not my fault it was a lovely view, and I stopped to admire it."

Granny Dottie chortled. "You'll have to take me along the next time. It's been a few years since I've seen a decent set of abs."

Grandpa Lucius kissed her cheek. "I might not have abs anymore, but I still know how to show you a good time."

I tried not to be grossed out by my grandparents smooching. It was sort of sweet in an old, wrinkly way. "If you think Blaze is cute, are you going to ask him out?" I asked Mom.

"Ooooh, that would make you a cougar," Auntie Queenie said and nudged me. "Your employee could become your step-father if he plays his cards right."

Mom blushed and swatted at me with a tea towel. "Of course not, but he's a charming young man. If you keep hiring staff who look like that, you're going to have a crowded bar every night."

"Full of middle-aged, lonely women looking for a good time," Auntie Queenie said.

I smiled at Mom. She hadn't dated since Dad had disappeared. She'd lost the love of her life and knew there was no point in trying to find a replacement.

"And how's that lovely young man, Axel?" Auntie Queenie said.

"His dad returned him yesterday," I said. "Axel seems good as new. In fact, when I saw him, it's as if he's had some improvements."

"What do you mean?" Mom asked.

"I can't put my finger on it, but he looks different. It's like his dad sent him for a makeover. He has a new haircut, and I'm sure his teeth look different. It's more than that; there's something about his energy. He felt stronger, more powerful." I'd only seen Axel for five minutes when he'd dropped by the bar yesterday. He'd thanked me for saving his life and had once again promised he wouldn't touch any mushrooms. I wasn't convinced but had been distracted by how different he'd seemed to scold him too much.

"His father is a powerful demon," Granny Dottie said. "Maybe he's decided he wants his son to step up into a more senior role."

I groaned. "Don't say that. I never want to find Axel on my hit list of demons who need hunting." That would be a conflict of interest I wouldn't know how to handle.

"What about your young man, Rhett?" Granny Dottie asked.

I stuffed a pancake into my mouth to avoid answering.

Everyone waited for me to chew my pancake, all eyes on me. This was something I'd been avoiding. I'd made my decision to save Rhett. I'd picked him over Axel, but I wasn't sure what it meant. A big part of me was way too scared to follow through after my initial actions. Maybe it meant nothing. I had to make a choice, so I did.

I swallowed the pancake and went to stab another with my fork, but Granny Dottie stopped me.

"Fine, I know he's doing okay. I saw Josh yesterday, and he filled me in."

"Don't you want to check that for yourself?" Auntie Queenie asked, a twinkle in her eyes.

I shrugged. Did I? If I followed through with my decision, it meant something big. Big, scary and possibly romantic.

"You shouldn't ignore Rhett," Mom chastised. "You go to all that effort to save his life and then don't bother to see how he's recovering."

"I've been busy. I have a business to run. I'm also recovering from being cursed."

"You're better now, and Cloven Hoof can look after itself for a few hours. You should go see Rhett today. He'll wonder if he's done something wrong."

"I'm eating breakfast!"

Mom grabbed my plate and replaced it with a large box. A sugar cinnamon scent drifted out of it. "You take these cookies to the boys and make sure they're doing okay."

"The boys?"

"Axel and Rhett. They both deserve cookies after what they've been through."

"Yum! Cookies." Wiggles' nose appeared on my knee.

"You've already eaten," I said to him.

"There's always room for cookies," Wiggles said.

"Now go," Mom said. "No dragging your heels."

"They will want to thank you," Granny Dottie said. "I bet they're grateful you saved their lives. You should have something in mind if they ask how they can repay you. I'd ask Axel for a new car and Rhett for a back rub and some hanky panky."

"You would." I glared at her for a second, but she just chuckled and ate a pancake.

"Go now." Mom pulled my chair back.

I reluctantly left the kitchen and headed outside with Wiggles, the box of cookies tucked under one arm.

"I think we should see Axel first and get that out of the way," Wiggles said.

"Good choice." Even though Axel was a notorious flirt, I never took him seriously. It would be good to see how he was doing and check out his new vibe again. There was something about it that set my teeth on edge. It had a dark edge I'd need to keep an eye on.

I headed to Axel's flash bachelor pad. The windows and doors were shut, and it looked like nobody was in. Before knocking on the door, I peeked through a ground-floor window.

"Oh my…"

Axel lounged on an enormous cream sofa. Leaning over him was a gorgeous blonde wearing a skimpy nurse's uniform. The hem of the outfit barely covered her panties.

Wiggles wolf whistled. "That's like no nurse I've ever seen. Is that uniform even legal? I can feel my blood pressure rising."

"It's definitely not. If she bends over, Axel might have a heart attack." I watched as the nurse popped a grape into Axel's mouth and ran a hand through his hair.

"We should go in," Wiggles said. "I have to be introduced to that nurse. I've got a stomach ache and need a belly rub."

"Another time." I backed away from the window carefully, not wanting to disturb Axel's *recovery*.

After another few seconds of leering at the nurse, Wiggles followed me. "We're not going to see her, I mean, him?"

"Axel will be just fine." I shook my head and laughed. Trust Axel to hire a cute blonde to nurse him back to health.

"Axel doesn't need your mom's cookies to get over being cursed. He can enjoy the cookies that hot nurse has."

I nodded as I pulled out two cookies and passed one to Wiggles before eating my own.

"Now to Rhett's?"

I sighed. "I guess so."

We'd only taken a few steps before the ground rumbled. I clutched the box of cookies tighter and looked around.

"Have you broken wind?" I asked Wiggles as I was engulfed in a waft of rotten eggs.

"Not guilty, but I can smell it too. Sulphur."

My gaze narrowed. Somewhere nearby was a demon. The air shimmered in front of me, and Axel's dad appeared in a flash of red smoke.

I gazed up at him, his eyes black murky pools as he peered down at me. "I didn't think you liked Willow

Tree Falls."

Kroni grunted. "I can't say I do. But my son decided to return. I'm keeping an eye on him until he is fully recovered."

"He's doing well," I said. "You might like to give him half an hour. He's got company."

Kroni chuckled. "He always was a ladies' man. He mentioned your name a lot when he was recovering."

"We're friends."

"Nothing more?"

I shook my head. I did not want a demon like Kroni as my father-in-law. "Nothing more."

"That is for the best." Kroni picked something long and stringy from between his teeth. "Crypt witches can be difficult."

"We aim to please," I said.

Kroni snorted and used a talon to scratch his chin. "Although I do not approve of your demon hunting activities, my son spoke fondly of you. You hold a place in his heart. Make sure you don't abuse that."

"I have no plans to. As I said, we're friends. I treat my friends well." After my visit to Rhett's, I was planning a trip to Sprinkles to buy the biggest cake I could find. I owed Izzie a huge apology and everyone else at Cloven Hoof for pulling rank. I'd never doubt any of them again.

"As it should be." Kroni sniffed the air and eyed the box in my hands. "Because of that, you will get no trouble from me."

"That's good to know." I tightened my grip on the box. This demon was not having my cookies.

"There's a chance we'll meet one day outside of Willow Tree Falls. The angels are not fans of yours."

"And when we do meet?" Kroni tilted his head.

I sucked in a breath. "When we do, one of us will win."

His hand reached out, his talons stroking down a strand of my hair. "It will not be you. You are good at what you do but don't underestimate my power. You saw a tiny hint of it when I saved my son. I can make life very difficult for you."

"You could, but would you want to do that to one of your son's friends?" I refused to flinch as his talon clipped my ear.

"We can come to an agreement," Kroni said.

"I don't make deals with demons." I discounted the recent bargain I'd made with Frank. Desperate times called for desperate measures.

"My deal is, we stay out of each other's way."

It wasn't a bad offer. I was sure I wouldn't be able to beat Kroni if he turned nasty. "I'll consider it."

"I've watched you work outside of Willow Tree Falls. You have taken some of my friends."

I arched an eyebrow. "Your friends do bad things. They deserve to be taken."

"I could have stopped you. I almost did on several occasions. Perhaps now, I will not watch you so much. I will allow you to do your job, providing you do nothing to harm my son and stay out of my way."

I couldn't believe Kroni was bargaining with me. He must seriously overrate my powers, or maybe there was a soft side to this demon, just like his son.

"I'd appreciate you not watching me. It sounds a bit creepy."

He chuckled. "I've been called a lot worse than a creep. Do we have a deal?"

I nodded slowly. I had no plans to hurt Axel. He was a super annoying, sometimes sleazy friend, but still a friend. "If you don't get in my way when I'm taking down demons, I don't see there being a problem."

"Then it is agreed." Kroni held out his hand, a talon raised.

I grimaced. Why do demons have such an obsession with blood? To seal the agreement, we had to exchange blood. I carefully ran the tip of my finger over the top of his talon and felt the skin break. He sliced his own finger open, and we pressed skin together, our powers mingling before the deal was formally sealed, demon-style.

"Have a pleasant life, Demon Hunter," Kroni said.

"You too. Have a pleasant... demon existence."

Kroni nodded, snatched the box of cookies from my hand, and vanished in a puff of red smoke.

"Hey! He stole the cookies." Wiggles growled at the spot Kroni had been standing.

I stared at my empty hand. "Typical demon. They always have a sweet tooth."

"Kroni always was a show off," Frank muttered in my head.

"Don't say you wouldn't do the same thing," I said as we headed back along the lane toward Rhett's house, minus my cookie gift.

"I'd do it with much more class."

"Could he beat me in a fight?" I asked Frank.

"Between the two of us, we could knock him on his fiery behind."

I snorted a laugh. Today was full of surprises. "You're suggesting we work together?"

"No, I'm suggesting I take advantage of you at every opportunity. Remember who I am. Remember why I'm here."

I pressed my lips together. Of course, Frank's focus was getting to Aurora. I could never let my guard down and take the risk that he would succeed.

"If you walk any slower, you'll go backwards." Wiggles turned and looked at me over his shoulder.

I was dragging my heels, but I didn't have a clue what to say to Rhett. I'd picked him. When backed into a corner, Rhett had been my choice. Did that mean I wanted to take it any further?

I arrived at his house and stood outside his front door, staring at it. "Maybe he's not in."

"Unless you knock, we'll never know," Wiggles said.

I knocked quietly. "See, he's not in."

Wiggles jumped up the door and pounded against it with his paws.

"Traitor!"

"Anything for true love and snacks. I bet Rhett has snacks."

Rhett pulled open the door and smiled when he saw me. "I've been hoping you'd drop by."

Other than looking a little paler than usual, Rhett was back to his frustratingly gorgeous self. "I wanted to give you time to recover after the incident in the forest."

"You mean the incident where you saved my life?" He grinned at me.

I nodded. "I had cookies to give you. They got stolen."

"Who stole them?"

"Axel's dad."

Rhett peered over my shoulder. "Kroni's here?"

"Not anymore. Neither are the cookies."

"No problem. I have cookies."

"I knew he would." Wiggles barged past him. "Show me the cookies."

Rhett shook his head as he watched Wiggles walk along the hallway. "I guess that means you're coming in."

"I guess so." I stepped through the doorway and looked around. "You've got some new pieces."

Rhett gestured at the small metal sculpture of a tortured angel. "A commission from a customer."

I inspected the begging, terrified expression on the sculpture's face. "Someone who does not like angels?"

Rhett chuckled. "Client confidentiality, but it's safe to say they run on the dark side. Come through. I've been working on something I think you'll both like." He led the way into the kitchen and gestured to a sculpture by the back door. "What do you think?"

I stared at the sculpture. "Is that…" I moved closer. "You've done a sculpture of Wiggles?"

Wiggles raised his head from his focused investigation of Rhett's trash. "Say what?"

"Get over here and take a look." Rhett had done an incredible job of capturing the slightly cocky, slightly surprised look Wiggles had on his face when he'd been caught doing something he shouldn't. His head was tilted, and he had one paw raised.

"I always see him doing that when he wants whatever you're eating." Rhett came to stand beside me. "Is it a good likeness?"

"It's incredible."

"You've captured my best features." Wiggles stood by the sculpture and raised a paw. "What do you think?"

Rhett laughed. "It's like you posed for me."

"Why would you make a sculpture of Wiggles?" I asked.

"When I see him trotting around the village, it reminds me of you." Rhett bent and brushed a speck of dust from the sculpture.

I glanced at him. "That's a good thing?"

"It could be. After all, I owe you one. You did save my life."

"I was helping the angels." I moved away from the sculpture, suddenly aware of how close Rhett was to me.

Rhett petted the head of the sculpture and then Wiggles. "How about some coffee?"

"And cookies?" Wiggles asked. "And a bowl of milk."

Rhett spent a few minutes brewing coffee and placed a bowl of milk down for Wiggles alongside a couple of cookies.

I sat at his counter not sure what to say. I couldn't deny I had feelings for Rhett, but they were complicated, and I'd been the one to walk away. But having experienced the gut wrenching fear of what it would be like to lose Rhett, it had made me pause. I wasn't ready to let him go. Maybe I should never have let him go.

Rhett placed a plate with cookies on in front of me. "You're quiet. Is there something on your mind?"

I grabbed a cookie and stuffed it in my mouth. "No, it's nothing."

Rhett twirled a strand of my hair around a finger. "There has been something playing on my mind."

"What's that?" I said around the cookie.

"I spoke to the guys after I got out of the forest. They filled me in on what happened. The fight with Kroni, the near miss in the shallow grave. All of it."

I nodded. "It was quite some fight."

"Not the fight. The fact that you got to me first." Rhett's gaze turned intense.

"I had to make a choice. It's not a big deal." I was such a liar.

"You chose me." He set his mug down and stared into my eyes. "You picked me over Axel."

I looked away and studied the sculpture of Wiggles. "I had a Plan B to save Axel."

"Oh, yeah. I heard about your Plan B. Kroni took out half the forest."

"Axel's dad is something else," I said. "But we've come to an agreement. He won't be a problem."

Rhett's shoulders stiffened. "He didn't mess with you?"

"He might have played a little, and he stole the cookies, but for a crazed demon, he was surprisingly reasonable."

"You have a dangerous job, Tempest."

"I'm used to it," I said. "I'm not going to change what I am or what I do, not for anybody." I raised my mug to my mouth.

Rhett eased the mug out of my grip before I could take a sip. "I didn't ask you to. But I still want to know why you picked me first."

I couldn't meet his gaze, knowing I'd give in if I did. "Maybe you were closer."

"No, it's not that. I've been back to the forest with the guys and taken a look around. Admit it. You wanted to save me."

"Of course! I didn't want to see you die."

Rhett chuckled. "That's about the best compliment I'm ever going to get from you."

I shrugged. "You have nice eyes." Rhett knew how gorgeous he was and how tempting he was to me. He didn't have to throw it in my face.

"So do you, when you look at me." He tapped a finger against the back of my hand. "What can we do about this situation we're in?"

I took a breath and stared at him. Nice eyes! I could lose myself for hours in those sexy, dark pools. "You know it's complicated."

"I know you're complicated. And I know you come with a hell of a lot of baggage. Who doesn't? I've got a past, and my future isn't going to follow the straightest of paths. We both have issues."

"We should go into therapy, not start dating."

"There's no fun if you don't have a few issues." A smile spread across Rhett's face. "Is that what you want, to start dating again?"

I blushed and looked away. "My main issue lives inside me. How do you feel about dating a demon?"

"If he comes attached to the gorgeous, headstrong, clever witch sitting in front of me, I don't have a problem." Rhett stepped closer. "I never have. You've always been the one to hold back."

"I never held back." I swallowed. He smelled so good, like a forest with a hint of engine oil. It was a perfect combination. "I just want everybody to stay safe."

Rhett tilted my chin up. "I can keep myself safe."

Wiggles cleared his throat. "Do I need to leave the room? If so, I'm taking some cookies to go."

Rhett laughed. "No, you stay where you are. You're going to have to get used to seeing this." He leaned forward and kissed me.

I should have resisted. I shouldn't have let myself sink into that kiss and forget how tricky a relationship with Rhett would be, but I didn't. Instead, I grabbed him by the collar and pulled him closer.

Wiggles groaned. "I'm out of here. You two are embarrassing."

I finally let go of Rhett when I became dizzy from lack of air and grinned up at him.

"Wow! That was quite a kiss." He traced a finger down my cheek. "What am I going to do with you, Tempest?"

"Accept me, demon and all."

"I always have. I want you in my life. I know it's never easy with you, and I know you'll always focus on your demons and keeping your sister safe above all else, but that's enough. Admit it. We're great together. You have to stop resisting me."

My gaze ran over Rhett. "It's not been easy. You do look great on your bike."

"There's room on the back if you ever want to ride with me." He pulled me in for another heart melting kiss.

I couldn't hold back any more. I liked Rhett. I liked him a lot. If this was going to work, I'd have to figure out how to date without Frank getting in the way.

I could do it. I could handle my demon, keep Aurora safe, and have Rhett in my life.

Rhett pulled back from the kiss and rested his forehead against mine. "So, Tempest Crypt, what next?"

I grinned up at him. "That's for us to decide together."

About Author

K.E. O'Connor (Karen) is a cozy mystery author living in the beautiful British countryside. She loves all things mystery, animals, and cake (these feature in her books.)

When she's not writing about mysteries, murder, and treats, she volunteers at a local animal sanctuary, reads a ton of books, binge watches mystery series on TV, and dreams about living somewhere warmer.

To stay in touch with the fun mysteries, where the killer always gets caught, justice is served magic style, and the familiars talk, join her newsletter.

Newsletter:
www.subscribepage.com/cozymysteries
Website: www.keoconnor.com/writing
Facebook: www.facebook.com/keoconnorauthor

Also By

Luck of the Witch

Hell of a Witch

Revenge of the Witch

Curse of the Witch

Son of a Witch

Framing of the Witch

Trickery of the Witch

Wishes of the Witch

Harmony of the Witch

Remedy of the Witch

Gift of the Witch

Toil of the Witch

Jinxing of the Witch

Craving of the Witch

Union of the Witch

Chaos of the Witch

Sleighing of the Witch

If you enjoyed

Revenge of the Witch

turn the page to read an extract from the next Crypt
Witch Mystery

CURSE OF THE WITCH

ISBN: 978-1-915378-02-6

Chapter 1

I stretched my legs under the oak kitchen table and leaned back in my seat. I yawned loudly and gave a grateful nod as Mom placed a large mug of black coffee in front of me.

She sighed and shook her head, a mournful look on her face. "I just cleaned this kitchen floor." My dusty, gooey footprints led in from the hallway.

I took a long sip of coffee. "Sorry, I needed some downtime after finishing work and knew the perfect place to come." I patted the demon catching bag hanging from my black belt loop. It carried a particularly pesky demon I'd been tracking outside Willow Tree Falls for three long, stressful days. He'd not come quietly, but they rarely did. This spiteful demon had also showered me in bright green slime as he'd fought to stay out of my bag.

"You can also blame me for the visit," Wiggles said from his seated position by my knee. "I heard you were baking some peach cobblers. That's my favorite. Cora, you make the best cobbler."

I grinned at him. So long as it was sweet, it was Wiggles' favorite food. My hellhound had such a sweet tooth.

"You're right. I am making cobbler," Mom said. "There's none for you. It's for the party."

I tilted my head, hoping I'd not forgotten anyone's birthday. "Whose party?"

"Don't tell me it's not on your calendar." Mom smiled. "It's the highlight of your auntie's year."

I straightened in my seat. "It's not her birthday, is it?"

Mom flapped a dishcloth at me. "Of course it isn't. It's the thirtieth reunion of your auntie's biker gang. They're all arriving. In fact, she's out right now collecting two of them."

I sipped more coffee, slowly relaxing now I was home and safe, and no demon was trying to gouge my favorite body parts. I had forgotten about the reunion party. Auntie Queenie used to run with the Dead Tree Witch biker gang. The gang was a force to be reckoned with in Willow Tree Falls, but that was a long time ago. They had a reunion every year and made a special effort every ten years to celebrate the trouble they'd gotten into over the decades.

"She's been looking forward to this for months."

"Auntie Queenie will have a great time. It's the rest of us who'll suffer," I said.

Mom chuckled as she checked the contents of the oven. "It's only right your auntie gets to blow off steam now and again."

"It's how much steam she blows off that's the problem. Do you remember their twentieth anniversary reunion? They destroyed the fountain outside the mayor's house."

Mom twisted her mouth to the side. "It wasn't so much destroyed as permanently altered."

"Fountains aren't supposed to spurt flames!"

Mom laughed. "I do remember the mayor's face when he woke the next morning to find rivulets of fire dripping from his mermaid's urn."

"They never confessed to it, but it had to be them."

"She's promised they'll all be on their best behavior. And they're getting on a bit, so I can't imagine they'll be too much trouble."

Auntie Queenie was Mom's older sister, but she wasn't that old. She was in her late fifties but acted like a woman half her age.

"I hope I'm like the gang when I'm that age." They still acted like excited teenagers most of the time.

"I'm sure you will be. Although, the last time they met, Bastille complained of a lingering throat infection, and Samantha mentioned a sore hip. We can all be young at heart even when the body starts to misbehave."

Dodgy hips or not, these witches were a handful. But their parties were always great, and they were fun to hang out with, always telling incredible stories about what they got up to when they were in the gang.

"We're back!" Auntie Queenie called from the hallway. She bustled into the kitchen, a big smile on her face. Behind her were Esmeralda DuPont and Lila Beaumont.

Esmeralda was tall, thin, and pale with a sharp face and jet-black hair that I was certain she dyed.

Lila was a few years older and had a shock of ice-white hair that sat around her head in a fluffy cloud. She always had a smile on her plump face and a twinkle in her blue eyes.

Mom hurried over and hugged them both. "I hope you had pleasant journeys."

"Mine was fine." Esmeralda kissed her cheek and smiled at me.

"I can't understand why you don't remain in Willow Tree Falls all the time," Auntie Queenie said. She passed by my seat and ruffled the top of my hair.

"I love my commune too much," Lila said. "Us single witches need to stick together. The commune is a peaceful place, where we hone our skills and aren't bothered by others." Lila specialized in healing and water magic and had an affinity with the sea. Her commune was a short walk to a beautiful beach with long stretches of pristine sand and warm salt water pools you could bath in.

Auntie Queenie huffed as she took a bottle of brandy from the shelf and waved it in the air. "Is it too soon?"

"Not for me," Lila said.

"Lovely! I'll have some in my coffee," Esmeralda said as she took a seat at the table. "The old place hasn't changed. Queenie walked us around before we came here."

"It's the same as always." Auntie Queenie passed around large brandies and coffee. "You're still in that drafty old cottage on the moors?"

Esmeralda nodded. "It's not drafty. It's cozy. I get no interference from other people."

"It must get lonely out there on your own." Mom settled at the table with everybody and placed a plate of homemade chocolate chip cookies in the center.

"I'm actually thinking about downsizing," Esmeralda said as she took a cookie.

"There's always a place for you in Willow Tree Falls," Auntie Queenie said. "It could be like old times if you come back."

"My knees won't take kindly to riding on a bike," Esmeralda said. "I have trouble getting my leg over these days."

Lila snorted coffee across the table. "So do I!"

The three women cackled with laughter.

"You can ride pillion with me," Auntie Queenie said as she topped up the glasses.

Lila chuckled. "That would be a sight. Two aging biker chicks raising hell in Willow Tree Falls."

"Less of the aging," Auntie Queenie said. "I've got plenty of good years in me."

I sat back and listened to their good-natured banter. It was always the same when the gang got back together. It seemed like no time had passed. They were quick to catch up with recent news and then spent the rest of the time reminiscing about the good old days when their gang ruled Willow Tree Falls.

"You need to watch what you say." Auntie Queenie lifted her chin in my direction. "Tempest is in with the enemy these days."

I frowned at her. "What do you mean?"

"She's dating Rhett Blackthorn." Auntie Queenie's voice lowered to a conspiratorial whisper.

"That gang is still around." Esmeralda sniffed in disapproval. "Maybe we should re-form and run them out of the village once and for all."

"It's a different crew these days," Auntie Queenie said. "Tempest's dating the leader."

I waved a hand in front of my face. "It's early days with Rhett. You can say whatever you like in front of me. It won't get back to him." It had been three months since I'd helped rescue Rhett from a curse. A curse that almost killed him. After his brush with death, I realized I had strong feelings for him and wanted to see where our relationship went. So far, it had gone well. We'd been on numerous dates, and I enjoyed his company. The kissing wasn't bad either.

But we were taking it slowly. I wasn't letting the fact my heart beat fast whenever I was around him affect my judgment. And I had history with Rhett and a pesky demon living inside me who stirred up trouble at inappropriate times. Dating was difficult when you came with a dark shadow, but Rhett was understanding.

"We'll make sure not to talk about our revenge plots against Rhett and his gang." Lila winked at me.

"Talk away. That gang can be trouble, but they're mainly harmless."

"It used to be a much rougher crowd," Auntie Queenie said.

"So bad they ran us out of the village," Esmeralda said.

There were disapproving mutters from Auntie Queenie and Lila about that unfortunate truth.

"I'm sure they used underhanded tactics," Auntie Queenie said. "And they caught us at a weak moment. Only cowards do that."

Mom tactfully cleared her throat. She'd seen many times how angry Auntie Queenie and her former gang members got when they discussed losing their place in Willow Tree Falls. "What plans have you got to celebrate this year?"

"We're having a party in the forest," Auntie Queenie said. "I've cleared it with Suki and Fallon. They're fine with it so long as we don't cause any damage and put out the fire."

Suki and Fallon were the wood nymphs who looked after our forest. It wasn't any old forest. It was full of magic and used to store powerful magical items that were best kept out of people's way because of their destructive qualities.

"I've ordered plenty of food from Bite Me," Auntie Queenie said.

"I'm glad we're going sophisticated this time," Esmeralda said. "I'm not a fan of pizzas and hotdogs like you provided last time."

"I always say you can do the catering if you don't like it," Auntie Queenie said. "I thought we'd have something with a bit of pizzazz, given it's been thirty years since we got together."

The three women all looked at each other and grinned like excited school kids.

"It doesn't seem like more than a few years since we were all here," Lila said. "How can time go so fast?"

Esmeralda leaned forward, her eyes sparkling. "I've still got my bike in storage. I can't part with the old girl, even though I don't ride anymore."

"You should have brought her with you," Auntie Queenie said. "It would have been great to take her for a spin for old times' sake."

"You're not allowed to ride," Mom said. "Our magic barrier can only sustain so many hits."

Auntie Queenie clicked her tongue against the roof of her mouth. "That was an accident. I don't know why people bring that up. I can still ride if I have to."

"What's that you've got in your bag?" Lila pointed to the demon bag that hung from my belt.

"Tempest is still doing freelance demon hunting work for the angels," Auntie Queenie said. She nodded at my bag. "Have we got company?"

"We have but not for long," I said. "I only got back a few hours ago. I needed to recharge my batteries before facing the angels."

"Have you got anyone interesting in there?" Lila leaned closer, her eyes glistening with interest.

"No one you'd like to meet," I said. "He's a sneaky one. He had me on the run for three days before I tracked him to a back alley behind an exotic dance bar."

Auntie Queenie shook her head. "What is it with these demons? They're either obsessed with girls dancing in sparkly thongs or lurking around takeout places. You'd think they'd have better things to do, like try to take over the world. But no, all they're interested in is fast food and fast women."

"Which is handy for me," I said. "I know where to look, and I can grab some food after I've captured them."

"Let me take a peek," Lila said. "I haven't had a rumble with a demon for years." Her hand inched toward the bag.

"Best if we don't let a demon loose in Mom's kitchen." I kept a tight hold on the bag.

"I'll smack him down if he makes a scene." Lila's hand moved closer.

Mom jumped up and hurried to my chair, placing a barrier between me and Lila. "Tempest, it's time you left. You've got that demon to deal with, and you must get cleaned up before you meet Caprice, Samantha, and Bastille."

I slid her a sideways glance. I was grateful for the rescue from Lila's inquisitive hand but hadn't realized I was getting lumbered with collection duties for the rest of Auntie Queenie's gang. "Can't they find their own way here?"

Mom pulled my chair back and shooed me toward the door. "No, that's not polite. You meet them at the barrier and show them to the hotel."

"Someone needs to keep an eye on them," Auntie Queenie said. "Those three are trouble when they get together."

"We'll see you at the party." Mom ushered me into the hallway.

I stopped when we were by the door and out of earshot of the others. "What gives? Why are you so keen to get me out of here?"

Mom glanced over her shoulder. "Lila loves demons."

"She does?"

"The last time they were here, I caught her snooping around the cemetery, looking for a crack. She wanted to meet a demon, test her skills, and make sure they hadn't gotten rusty. I was worried she'd let out that demon you're carrying. I can't have that. He might destroy my peach cobblers."

I arched an eyebrow. "That would be a crime."

"It absolutely would." Wiggles wandered out of the kitchen, his mouth full of something that looked suspiciously like peach cobbler.

Mom tilted her head and tutted. "Go on. Get out of here you two. And wipe some of that goo off your clothes, or they'll think I raised a wildling."

I looked down and shrugged as I saw the stains on my outfit. "It's a part of the job."

"Your auntie's friends will think I don't look after you properly."

I kissed her cheek. "Mom, I can take care of myself. What time do I need to meet the rest of auntie's party?"

REVENGE OF THE WITCH

Mom checked the time and gasped. "Five minutes! They're arriving by the Green Man."

"Then I'd better get a move on." I hurried out of the house with Wiggles. There was no time for a change of clothes or clean-up of any kind. They'd have to take me as they found me. It wouldn't be the first time they'd seen me smeared in some kind of gross demon residue.

Wiggles trotted along beside me as I broke into a jog. "I love Queenie's reunions. They always know how to party."

"You only love them because they give unlimited belly rubs," I said.

"They have their priorities right," Wiggles said. "Party hard, treat a hellhound right, and have fun."

"Let's make a quick detour. I need to dump this demon before we meet the others just in case they get interested in trying to set him free, as well."

We changed direction and jogged to Angel Force's headquarters. It was a huge, white building in the center of the village.

I pushed through the door to find Dazielle at the desk, talking to Cassiel.

"One demon, all yours." I unclipped the bag from my belt and handed it to Dazielle.

"Good work." She passed the bag to Cassiel, who vanished out the back to decant him into a safe container. "I hear your auntie's having a party tonight."

"Good news spreads fast. Don't be offended if your invitation got lost in the post." Dazielle had a habit of accusing Auntie Queenie of things she hadn't done, and there was no love lost between them.

Dazielle smirked. "Tell her to be careful. I know what she's like."

"She knows how to have fun. There's nothing wrong with that."

"Even so, keep an eye on her and her misbehaving friends. I don't need a bunch of overexcited, middle-aged witches causing havoc in Willow Tree Falls."

"There might be a little havoc, but I'll see if I can keep a lid on things."

Cassiel returned and handed me my now empty bag.

"Make sure you do," Dazielle said. "I'll arrest them for disorderly conduct if things get out of hand."

"That'll look good in the local paper: Police Chief Harasses Overexcited Middle-Aged Witches Reunion Shocker!!!"

Dazielle sniffed. "I'll treat them the same as anyone else if they break the law."

"You should come to the party," Wiggles said, "so long as you promise not to be a party pooper. I'll see if I can get you in."

"I have better things to do than hang out with a bunch of eccentric witches," Dazielle said.

"Washing your hair?" I asked.

Her eyes narrowed. "Maybe. But I might drop by to make sure they aren't causing problems."

"We look forward to it. If you're bringing nibbles, we're low on salty snacks." I shook my head as we headed out of the building. Auntie Queenie would not want any angels at her party ruining the vibe.

I raced to the edge of the magic barrier where a broken hunk of green stone, known to locals as the Green Man, rested against a lightning struck oak.

I was just in time to see three women emerge. Their images looked misty as they passed through the magic.

Samantha Smythe-Barrow was easy to spot. She was a curvy witch with flame red hair and green eyes. She carried her fifty-five years well and often caught men's attention.

Bastille Drew was next. She'd always been the quiet one of the group. She had a neat gray bob, a fondness for long cardigans, and lots of silver rings.

Caprice Gray was the final arrival, with a neat dark pixie cut, a willowy figure, and intense dark eyes.

They all waved at me as I approached.

"Tempest, it's lovely to see you." Samantha air kissed either side of my cheeks. She was the refined one of the group until she'd had a few drinks.

"We've been so looking forward to our visit," Caprice said. "Where's Queenie?"

"Entertaining Esmeralda and Lila," I said. "She asked me to take you to the hotel."

"Lovely, and you must join us later on." Caprice grabbed my elbow and walked alongside me. "We're going to have such fun."

"I'll definitely drop by," I said.

"You must stay all night," Caprice said. "I want to hear all your news."

"Watch out. I spot trouble." Samantha grabbed Caprice and Bastille's arms and yanked them to a stop, her gaze narrowing as she stared across the street.

I looked over to where she was staring, and my eyes widened. Rhett and his entire gang sat astride their bikes in a single line of leather-clad menace. They hadn't been there when I'd hurried past a moment ago.

"If they're trying to intimidate us, it's failing." Caprice lifted her chin and stared them down. "They're little boys on big bikes that they don't know how to handle."

"They're fine," I said. "Give me a minute, though, and I'll make sure they're not after anything."

"They'll find my foot whacking them in the backside if they spoil our fun," Caprice hollered, loud enough so they could all hear.

I hurried over to Rhett, hoping the blush I felt hadn't spread to my cheeks. "You look like you mean business."

"Just making sure our new arrivals are appropriately welcomed." Rhett grinned at me and winked.

"Your gang rivalry was a long time ago, before you were head of this gang," I said.

"It's tradition when former gang members arrive in the village. It never hurts to remind them who's in charge," Rhett said. "We might be the new generation, but old grudges stick."

I shook my head. "Look at them. They're middle-aged women. They—"

"Incoming!" Josh yelled.

Rhett grabbed me and yanked me against his chest as something hot and magic-laced shot past us.

"Sorry!" Samantha shouted. "My aim's a little off."

I peered over Rhett's shoulder to see a flaming purple rock behind us. I turned toward her. "A little! You almost took my head off."

"See what I mean?" Rhett brushed my dark hair off my face, amusement glinting in his eyes. "They might have a few wrinkles, but those witches have power. They're not our fans, so we return the favor."

I nodded, my attention shifting to his mouth. "They won't be a problem. They're only here for a couple of days."

"They might be. Those witches have a lot of power, especially when they get together." Rhett's gaze moved over my shoulder, and his fingers tightened on my back.

I turned to see Caprice shoot a green flame into the air, her glare fixed on the gang.

I groaned and rubbed my forehead. "Okay, so they're powerful witches. They still won't cause you any trouble. They're here to get merry, drink too much, and talk about old times."

Rhett scrubbed his stubbled chin before nodding. "Are we still on for tomorrow night?"

I grinned at him. "Of course. Tonight, I have to take care of this lot, but I'm free tomorrow." Rhett had asked to take me stargazing. I wasn't sure I'd enjoy it, but if it meant alone time with Rhett, snuggled on a blanket, I was willing to experiment.

"I'll pick you up at ten. We won't get the best view until midnight."

"Not a problem." I glanced at the other members of his gang, who were watching the three witches with scowls on their faces, before giving him a quick kiss. "See you tomorrow."

I felt the urge to skip as I hurried away from Rhett. It was silly, but he always made me feel like a teenage girl with a giant crush.

Caprice shot another bout of flame into the air, and Samantha and Bastille laughed as I drew near.

I doused the flames with my own magic. "That's enough showing off."

Caprice raised her neat eyebrows at me. "You're having a dalliance with Rhett Blackthorn?"

I shrugged. "Sort of."

"What does Queenie think about that?" Samantha asked.

"If I'm happy, she's happy. Do you have an issue with who I date?"

Samantha laughed. "When he's as hot as that, of course not. It's just a shame he runs that rabble."

I turned and smiled at Rhett. "They aren't so bad when you get past the attitudes."

"I'm itching to try out my new ice spell," Caprice said. "I should see if these big, tough guys fancy a little frost on their beards."

"No! No frost on anything." I blew out a breath. "Let's get to the hotel."

"Just a little spell," Caprice said. "I promise not to hurt any of them." Ice danced across the ground toward the bikers.

"Wiggles." I pointed at the ice.

He sucked in a breath and belched out a hot steam of brimstone laced smoke, melting the ice.

"Oh, you're no fun, you bad puppy." Caprice pouted.

Wiggles shrugged. "I had trapped wind. If I hold it in, I get a stomach ache."

Caprice frowned. "I'm still keeping an eye on that gang. I don't trust them."

"No one does." I tilted my head in the direction of the hotel. "Let's get a move on. You don't want to be late for the fun."

These witches might be retired from the gang, but they were still a big handful of mischief.

Curse of the Witch is available in paperback and e-book.

ISBN: 978-1-915378-02-6